Ron. a 2022 Book.

*New York Times* and *USA Today* bestselling novelist **MARY BURTON** is the popular author of more than thirty-eight romance and suspense novels as well as five novellas. She currently lives on the Outer Banks of North Carolina with her husband and three miniature dachshunds. Visit her at www.maryburton.com.

GW00542304

# Also by Mary Burton

*Find You*
*Playing With Fire*

# Keep You Close

## MARY BURTON

ONE PLACE. MANY STORIES

HQ
An imprint of HarperCollins*Publishers* Ltd
1 London Bridge Street
London SE1 9GF

www.harpercollins.co.uk

HarperCollins*Publishers*
1st Floor, Watermarque Building, Ringsend Road
Dublin 4, Ireland

This paperback edition 2022

1

First published in Great Britain as *In Dark Waters* by
MIRA 2011

This edition published in Great Britain by HQ,
an imprint of HarperCollins*Publishers* Ltd 2022

Copyright © Mary Burton 2011

Mary Burton asserts the moral right to be
identified as the author of this work.
A catalogue record for this book is
available from the British Library.

ISBN: 9781848459021

MIX
Paper from
responsible sources
FSC C007454

This book is produced from independently certified FSC™ paper
to ensure responsible forest management.

For more information visit: www.harpercollins.co.uk/green

# Chapter 1

Kelsey Warren arrived at the gated entrance of Diamond Stone Quarry just after sunrise.

She ignored the No Trespassing sign, opened the shiny, new aluminum gate and drove down the winding dirt road until it dead-ended into a freshly bulldozed parking area. From the lot, an extra wide access ramp led to the flooded quarry.

Fresh rays of sun glistened on the quarry's smooth waters and bounced up rocky, straight slopes. Despite the dawning light, the waters looked cold and eerily dark. This was a dive she'd have gladly skipped. She always preferred diving in the warm waters of the Caribbean or South Pacific to quarries. If her old friend Stu Hamilton hadn't asked her to dive as a favor, she'd already be on her way to Dulles Airport to catch the next flight to L.A.

She stopped her car and sat back, letting her head fall back against the seat's leather headrest. At one time, the played-out quarry had been the lifeblood of this region of Virginia. In its heyday, Diamond Stone had brought money, jobs and prosperity to Grant's Forge. But that had been long before she'd been born.

Why the devil did Stu want her to dive this quarry? She checked her watch. Six-twenty.

Stu was late.

Getting out of her car, she walked to the tailgate of the rented yellow Jeep and opened it. She tugged a large canvas duffel bag toward her and unzipped it as she kicked off her well-worn brown clogs. Years of teaching scuba to tourists with no sense of time had taught her to prep her gear as much as she could ahead of time. She slid off her faded jeans and black shirt, revealing a blue bikini.

Kelsey pulled out her wet suit, tugged it over her hips, slid her arms inside and zipped it up just past her belly ring. She laid out a bright blue tarp, arranged her dive gear and underwater camera on it.

Sitting cross-legged on her tarp, she checked her watch again. Six thirty-five.

It wasn't like Stu to be late. He wasn't a tourist, but a businessman who prided himself on punctuality.

Kelsey shifted her focus back to the still waters. Hard to believe that less than a week ago she'd been in Fiji photographing surfers on the reefs near Beaqua Island. That Tuesday had gone particularly well. She'd not only shot a lionfish, but a school of barracuda as well. To top it off, the satellites had been working and she'd been able to email the digital photos to her editors at *Travel* and *National Geographic*.

But the day that had started so well had soured quickly when Stu had called and told her that her aunt had suffered a stroke. Kelsey and her aunt hadn't been close. The old woman had resented having a fifteen-year-old dumped into her life and she never missed a chance to say so. But when Kelsey's mother, Donna, had taken off for good that last time, Ruth had kept Kelsey with her. *The decent thing to do*, Ruth had always said. Whatever the reasons, Ruth's intervention had meant no foster care. And as much as Kelsey had hated her sour aunt's face, she despised the system more. To her way of thinking, she owed Ruth one last show of respect. So she left Fiji to attend Ruth's funeral.

But getting back to the States had proven more difficult than she'd imagined. Kelsey had had to wait two days before she could catch a fishing boat to take her to the main island and then another day before she could board a plane to the States. After forty-eight hours of flying and numerous layovers later, she'd arrived early yesterday in Grant's Forge, Virginia. Three hours too late for Ruth's funeral.

Kelsey closed her eyes. She could almost hear Ruth now. "A day late and a dollar short. No good, just like your mother."

To her amazement, tears pooled in her eyes. It had been eight years since she'd seen Ruth and ten years since Donna had ditched her, yet memories of both women had the power to crush the air from her lungs.

A tear ran down her cheek.

Ruth's dour nature could be explained away by age, but Kelsey had never figured out why her mother had taken off that last time. Donna had left Kelsey before with neighbors and friends, but she'd never been gone more than a week. She'd always come back.

Until that last time.

A car sounded on the gravel road behind her, startling her from her thoughts. Wiping away the tears, she rose as a black Suburban parked next to Kelsey's Jeep. Painted on the side was Grant's Forge Sheriff.

Kelsey stiffened. Damn. The last thing she needed was trouble with the local sheriff. Sheriff Buddy Hollis had never missed an opportunity to razz her when she was growing up.

To her surprise, Stu got out of the Suburban's passenger side. Just under five foot six with a large belly, he wore a white tank top, cut-off shorts and tennis shoes. His thinning gray hair was tied back at the nape of his neck. The sun had etched deep lines into his face.

After she'd gone to the funeral home and discovered Ruth's service was over, she'd checked into a hotel room and crashed. She'd talked to Stu last night, but this was the first time she'd seen him in eight years. He hadn't changed a bit. She couldn't help but smile.

"I wasn't sure if you'd make it," he said, limping toward her. He gave her a big hug.

She melted into the strong embrace. Stu had written to her weekly for the last eight years. No matter where she was, his letters found her. He had always made her feel special. "I said I'd be here."

"You've been promising to come home for five years. I was beginning to think I'd never see you again."

Kelsey swallowed the tightness in her throat. Damn it, she wasn't going to cry. Sniffing, she glanced down at his bandaged foot. "What happened to you?"

He brushed her concern away with the wave of a hand. "Nothing. A stupid accident."

He was blowing her off and she was ready to call him on it when the driver's side of the Suburban opened. Mitch Garrett stepped out.

Broad shoulders stretched Mitch's faded blue T-shirt imprinted with the words Naval Academy on the front. Corded muscles strained beneath jeans that had seen better days. His black hair, cut regulation style, accentuated a square, unshaven jaw.

A knot tightened in Kelsey's chest.

*Mitch Garrett.*

Damn her luck. He'd been her first lover. And he was the last man she ever wanted to see again. This town was nothing but one bad memory after another.

Mitch shook his head as if he half expected her to vanish. He was just as shocked to see her as she him. Recovering, his gaze trailed slowly down her body and then back up to her face. He sized her up, and it didn't take a rocket scientist to figure he wasn't happy to see her.

"Kelsey Warren." The years had deepened his voice and made it rustier.

Every nerve in her body tensed. She itched to leave right now. Her palms felt damp. "I thought you went into the Navy." Damn.

4

After all this time, that was the best she could come up with. He'd definitely rattled her.

"I'm out."

"And you're the sheriff?" *Brilliant.* "Right."

In her daydreams, she'd always been clever and witty when she ran into Mitch Garrett again. Now, she could barely string two sentences together. "Stu, I'm unpacked and ready to go. Whenever you're ready, we can dive."

"Mitch didn't want me to chance a dive with the bad leg. He's gonna dive in my place."

"What?"

"Where's Chris?" Mitch demanded. "I thought *he* was diving with me today."

Stu shrugged, unmoved by their shocked expressions. "He's gone up to Atlantic City for a couple of days of gambling."

"He took off just like that?" Mitch said. "The guy's a great diver but a pain in the ass at times. Sometimes he leaves for a few days without notice. Usually, it's not a problem. Today it was. I'd have been in a bind if Kelsey and you hadn't agreed to dive."

Mitch's jaw tightened and then released. "Stu, I could have called one of my buddies from the Reserves."

"I figured with Kelsey in town, it didn't make sense to call in another diver. Sorta like old times for you two."

*Old times.* Kelsey nearly laughed. She and Mitch had met eight years ago when they'd both worked in Stu's dive shop. The job had been a way for Mitch to kill time during the summer months between college graduation and basic training. For her, it had been a lifeline that had kept her sane after her last year of high school. Mitch had been kind and respectful to her. She'd fallen in love with him. At the end of the summer, they'd ended up in bed.

Kelsey sighed. "You should have said something." Unmoved, Stu wrapped his arm around Kelsey's tense shoulders. "Relax, you two. I'm just asking for a half-hour dive, not a trip down the aisle."

Kelsey tensed. "Stu, I don't think this is going to work. The

5

sheriff doesn't want to dive with me, and frankly I'm not too fond of the idea myself."

A muscle pulsed in Mitch's jaw. Bull's-eye.

"I'll pack up my gear," she said. "He can call in another diver."

Stu sighed. "Kelsey, don't go."

"I didn't say I wouldn't dive with you," Mitch said tensely. He shook his head. "I'll get my gear."

Kelsey could cheerfully have strangled Stu right now. "You should have told me I was diving with Mitch," she said, her voice barely a whisper.

"I didn't think it mattered."

"It matters."

Mitch unpacked his equipment and moved toward them, a large silver air tank in one hand and a black duffel in the other. His posture was military straight. Every step was deliberate, precise. Tension tightened his muscles as he moved toward her.

The years had been good to him. Dark hair, with rawboned features, whipcord body and ice-blue eyes that missed little. Very masculine.

He set down his equipment beside hers. "How many places you lived these last few years?"

If he could keep this impersonal and pretend they'd never been lovers, so could she. "Lost count."

"You plan on sticking around here long?" He sounded as if he were checking the questions off a list.

She smiled, but there was nothing humorous about his question. "I doubt it."

Mitch lifted a brow. "I figured you'd stay long enough to settle Ruth's estate. Her house is worth good money."

"I didn't come back for the money." More tension crept into her voice. "I'm pretty successful, despite predictions that I'd not amount to much."

An unnamed emotion flickered in his eyes. "That's right, you're some successful photographer—a real hot ticket."

It almost sounded as if he'd kept up with her. Unreasonable pleasure bubbled inside her before she tamped it down. "If this small talk is for my benefit, Sheriff, you can skip it. I just want to do the dive and be on my way."

Irritation flashed in Mitch's blue eyes. "How long has it been since you've flown?"

Now, he questioned her competence. "I never dive within twenty-four hours of flying." That kind of sloppy mistake could lead to a burst blood vessel in the brain, heart or lungs.

"How long?" he said tensely.

Male divers had underestimated Kelsey before, but she always took it in stride. However, Mitch's attitude struck a nerve. *"Thirty-six hours."*

Stu's gaze darted between the two. "Kelsey's logged over a thousand hours. She's one of the best divers around."

Mitch lifted an eyebrow. "The best among the rich and famous?"

She didn't have to justify herself to anyone and yet here she stood ready to recite her résumé. She stopped herself. "You been in the water recently, Sheriff?" she asked tartly. "Not many dive opportunities in the mountains, I mean other than Stu's Dive Shop pool. I'll bet the fish Stu's painted on the bottom are very lifelike."

Mitch's gaze hardened. He had always hated a smart-ass, and he clearly hadn't changed. Once she'd watched him toss a guy out of the diner for mouthing off to a waitress. "I dove in the Atlantic three days ago."

"Mitch is in the Navy Reserves," Stu said. "Spent the last two weeks in the water off Norfolk."

Kelsey brushed back her hair with impatient fingers. Normally, she kept her emotions in check and it annoyed her that he'd gotten under her skin.

The annoyance in Mitch's eyes gave her a perverse sense of satisfaction. Good to know she could still worm under his skin, too. "Then suit up. We're already thirty minutes late."

He yanked off his T-shirt. Dark hair matted his hard, lean and well-muscled chest. When he reached for the snap of his jeans, she tore her gaze away and dropped it back to her gear. A frisson of desire shot through her limbs. From the corner of her eye, she saw he wore bathing trunks. Part of her was relieved, part disappointed.

Don't be dumb, Warren. Last time you got stupid with this man, you got burned.

Her mouth dry, she shifted her gaze to Stu. "Okay, Stu, why *are* we diving today?"

"I bought the quarry."

She lifted her brows. "Why?"

"I'm turning it into an open water dive training spot. There's a big demand for it. I plan to open next week."

She lifted a brow. "But?"

"We had the water filtered and Chris and I started surveying the spot last week. Two days ago, we found an old car perched on the lip of a ravine. If a tourist were to get tangled up in it, it would pull him down two hundred feet into the crevice."

She shrugged. "So you want Mitch and me to push it over into the ravine?"

"No," Mitch said. "I want to get the plates first and run them. If they're clean, I'll come back with Chris and take care of the car."

"You really think an old car is worth the trouble?" she said.

"I'm not fond of loose ends," Mitch said. She shrugged. "Whatever."

She rechecked her tank and the camera's waterproof case as he slipped on his dive suit. She doubted there'd be much to photograph in the quarry, but she always took her camera out of habit. Her best shots had materialized when she'd least expected them.

He strapped a knife to his leg and a dive computer to his wrist. Effortlessly, he lifted his tank and slipped it on.

Kelsey reached for her tank, ready to heft it onto her shoulders. But Mitch brushed her fingers aside and lifted her gear for her. For an instant, she was undecided. She didn't like receiving help, especially from this man. Still, to refuse would only delay this happy reunion longer. She quickly slipped her arms into the buoyancy compensator vest, which held air regulator hoses, air tank and dive computer in place. "Thanks."

Mitch hovered behind her and his thigh brushed her leg. He supported the weight of her tank as she fastened her straps. For an instant, her fingers fumbled with the straps she'd hooked a thousand times. "Any time."

Stu handed Kelsey her yellow fins and pink mask. "All set?" he asked.

She rechecked her handheld dive computer. "Good to go," she said tightly.

On land the equipment was cumbersome, but once they entered the water, the thirty-pound tank would be weightless.

Stu followed them down the hill to the water. "Now remember, the large crevice is near the northwest corner of the quarry. That's where I saw the car."

"We'll find your car," Mitch said. His face held no hint of emotion.

Mitch walked into the water, and when it was waist deep, he rolled easily on his back and yanked on his fins. He secured his mask and double-checked the airflow in his regulator.

Even this late in May, the water was ice-cold.

Kelsey sucked in a breath, determined not to say a word in front of Mitch. She slipped on her fins and pulled her hot pink mask in place. Placing her regulator in her mouth, she drew in a deep breath to test it.

Kelsey moved deeper into the water.

Mitch shot a glance her way. Her hot pink dive mask had him shaking his head. "Christ, Stu, my first day off in three weeks and you stick me with Scuba Barbie. You owe me, pal. You owe me big-time."

9

# Chapter 2

Mitch prayed for patience as he shoved the regulator into his mouth. Kelsey Warren hadn't lost her talent for getting under his skin.

The last time he'd seen Kelsey was eight years ago, when he'd had more hormones than sense. Back then, he hadn't seen past her wisecracks to the pain she hid so carefully. He had badly misjudged what he'd thought was an easygoing relationship.

They'd made love in the back room of Stu's Dive Shop. For him, it had been incredible until she'd told him that she was a virgin and that she'd loved him.

He'd been stunned.

He'd been honest and told her he didn't love her.

Like a fool, he'd added that he'd never have made love to her if he'd known. She'd looked horrified, and the sloppy apologies that had tumbled out of him one after another had made a painful situation even worse.

Kelsey had fled that back room in tears. He'd tried to follow, but she'd hopped in her car and taken off. He'd gone immediately to her aunt's house to see her. But she'd packed up her few belongings and had left. Her aunt didn't know where she'd gone and didn't seem to care. He never saw her again.

Until now.

Mitch exhaled slowly into the regulator. He was wiser now. This time, he would keep matters strictly business between them.

He pushed the regulator into his mouth, slid below the water's edge, and started to kick his fins. The cool waters felt good against his body. The tension bunching his muscles relaxed a fraction.

The water was cold, and flecks of silt kicked up from the bottom by their movement floated in the water around them. Still, the water had cleared significantly since Stu had put in the new filtration system. He could see almost a hundred feet ahead. Hard to believe six months ago, the visibility in the quarry had been less than two inches.

Mitch removed his flashlight from his waistband and switched it on. He swam ten feet above Kelsey, giving him a perfect view of her. She still had a tight, compact body and full, rounded breasts that filled out her skintight wet suit exactly right.

Her hair was blonder, the color of platinum, but if he didn't miss his guess, it was natural, the product of hours in the sun. Her blue eyes had spit fire the instant she'd looked at him, but he imagined if she smiled, they'd still have the power to make his knees weak. The bracelets that jangled from her wrist looked like quality, as did the gold chain that hung around her neck.

Over the last couple of years, Stu had kept him updated on Kelsey's whereabouts. Mitch had heard enough to know she was doing well. And judging by Stu's collection of postcards from Kelsey, she didn't stay in any one place long.

Yesterday, when they'd left the funeral home after Ruth Warren's service, Stu had defended Kelsey to the folks who'd wondered why she'd not returned for the occasion. Later at the diner over coffee, Stu had talked more about Kelsey. Donna's abandonment, he'd said, had left its mark on her.

Mitch knew Kelsey's upbringing had not been ideal, but he'd never known how bad things had been. That summer when they'd worked together, she'd never said a word about her family life.

11

He had never met Kelsey's mother, but in the years since he'd moved back home, he'd heard enough tales. Anyone in town older than thirty-five had a Donna Warren tale. The woman had lived hard and fast and abandoned her only child ten years ago. Mitch had been away at school, but from what he'd heard, it had been big news at the time.

He watched Kelsey aim her camera at a couple of fish. It flashed. As she turned and pointed her camera to the right, his flashlight cast a glow on her pink face mask. Blond hair floated behind her.

Small schools of fish hovered close to her head. One nibbled her ear. Turning, she held out her gloved hand and waited as the fish swam closer to her fingertips.

His mind drifted back to a time when their bodies had fit so well together. He wondered if the sex would still be as explosive. Lust pumped through his veins. At the rate he was going, he would burn through his air tanks in a half-hour.

Sleep was what he needed, not Kelsey.

He'd spent the last two weeks on active reserve duty in Norfolk. Most of the time was spent under the water, inspecting the hulls of the ships for explosives. He'd returned home on Friday, hoping for a couple of quiet days before he had to get back to work and plunge into planning his reelection campaign. No such luck.

Kelsey snapped a couple more pictures, turned and started swimming again.

A hundred feet ahead, he spotted a silhouetted object.

The car.

Mitch shifted his mind to business. Without looking back at him, Kelsey swam toward the car. She shot a couple of pictures of it.

No doubt, she'd photographed her share of exotic underwater creatures. He'd seen her pictures in several travel magazines. He'd even subscribed to a couple magazines last year so he could keep tabs on her work.

He'd bet next month's paycheck that she'd never shot an

abandoned heap. He could almost hear her mind grousing about her adventures in Hicksville as she counted off the minutes until she could leave Grant's Forge.

The old car sat perched on the edge of a deep crevice that dipped another two hundred feet. Another two or three feet and the car would have plunged to the bottom of the ravine and never have been found. Stu was right to be worried about it.

He moved alongside Kelsey.

Kelsey took another picture. They swam closer.

When they were just twenty feet away, Kelsey lowered the camera from her face mask. Abruptly, she started to swim fast toward the wreck.

Her keen interest in the old car surprised him. Water had corroded the paint off the vehicle and the windows were covered with slime. Water had seeped inside and flooded the interior. A Dodge, twenty years old if he had to guess.

She reached for the door handle and tried to open it. What the hell was she going to do? Swim in the car?

Mitch tapped her on the shoulder and she looked up at him. Her eyes were wide, bright. He shook his head and pointed to the ravine, a reminder she could be sucked over the edge if her equipment got hooked in the car and it tumbled over. Nodding, she released it.

She placed her hand against the opaque glass. She stared at the car a long moment before she swam toward the rusted back bumper. She unhooked a small light from her weight belt and shone it on the license plate.

He nudged her aside and rubbed the plate partially clean. Pennsylvania. ZCE A. The rest was unreadable, corroded away by the water, but it might be enough to get an ID.

Likely, the car had belonged to someone who didn't want to pay property taxes and had dumped the car here. But he'd run the plates anyway. So many crimes were solved by seemingly unimportant details.

Kelsey shouldered past him and started to clean the remaining numbers. When she realized the numbers couldn't be salvaged, she swam quickly back to the front driver's side of the car. This time, she started wiping furiously at the window until she'd cleaned off a small patch. She fumbled for her light and in the process dropped her camera. Unmindful that it sank to the silty bottom, she shone her light into the car.

Her body jerked. She pushed back from the car.

She turned toward him, her eyes wider. She was breathing harder, faster. Bubbles swirled around her head.

Something was wrong.

He stared at her. *What is it?*

She pointed to the Dodge.

Mitch shrugged. *What?*

She jabbed her finger at the window. *Look!*

He shone his flashlight into the car's interior. Through the thick, murky waters, he saw the skeleton draped across the front seat of the car, staring lifelessly through empty sockets at him.

Kelsey closed her eyes to block out the sight of the car that Donna had driven off in ten years ago. Pennsylvania plates. ZCE A. She didn't need the last three numbers to know that this had been her mother's car. Or that the skeleton was her mother.

*She knew.*

Tight bands of stress wrapped around her chest, squeezing the air from her lungs. A million thoughts ricocheted in her head. She started breathing faster.

Opening her eyes, she looked up toward the surface. The sun shone into the dark waters. She had to get out of the quarry as quickly as she could. She needed to stand on dry land. To think. Every instinct in her body screamed for her to claw her way to the surface. Instead, she closed her eyes and drew in deep, slow breaths.

*Take your time, Warren. Don't panic.* Her breathing slowed. She swallowed, her mouth dry. Mitch took a hold of her wrist. She was surprised by the gentleness in his touch. He was watching her intently now.

14

Finally, through watery eyes, she met his steely gaze and nodded. *I'm all right.*

His eyes narrowed. *Yeah, right.*

He didn't let loose of her arm as they floated up fifteen feet and then paused for their bodies to adjust to the new depth.

After a three-minute safety interval, Mitch ascended with Kelsey another fifteen feet and stopped. Though she'd stayed in control, his hand and gaze remained locked on her. When they'd waited another minute, he took them up another fifteen feet, and then up to the surface.

He jerked his head toward land. Silently he swam next to her until they reached shallow water.

*Donna was dead. Her mother was dead.*

The rush of adrenaline drained her body and by the time she reached the shore, she could barely stand. Stu started to make his way down the hill toward her. She gritted her teeth and stood in the shallow water, fighting the weight of the tank. Pebbles from the shore dug into her feet.

Very aware that Mitch watched her every move, she yanked off her fins. She staggered the ten feet through ankle-deep water to the shore. She dropped her tanks on the shore and closed her eyes, gathering her strength. Anyone could be in that car. In her heart, she knew it was Donna.

Stu's blue eyes had darkened with curiosity. "That was quick."

"Let me lift your tank off your shoulder," Mitch said gruffly.

She stood taller. "I'll take care of it."

Annoyed, he started to lift the tank from her body. "You look like you're about to collapse."

She drew in a deep steadying breath. "I'm fine."

Stu frowned. "What happened? Did you find the car?"

Mitch shrugged off his tanks. "Yeah. We found the car."

Stu's gaze skipped between Mitch's face etched with anger and Kelsey's pale features. "What went wrong?"

"There was a body in the car. A skeleton," Kelsey said.

"A what?" Stu asked.

She couldn't seem to catch her breath. "It was Donna's car."

"Jeez, Kelsey," Stu said. "Her blue Dodge?"

"Yeah."

Mitch eyed her. "Kelsey, it was dark down there, and the car was covered in slime. We don't know whose car it was or who was in it."

"I know what I saw! Donna's plates. 'You've Got A Friend In Pennsylvania!' Didn't you see it?"

Mitch shoved his fingers through his wet hair. "I saw the plates."

Her hands started to tremble. "The body is Donna's."

The wheels in Mitch's mind seemed to turn faster as if he were switching to full cop mode. "Kelsey, don't borrow trouble until I go down and check it out again."

"Mitch is right, Kelsey," Stu said. "It could be anyone."

All the fears and emotions of ten years ago roared to life, tearing at her heart. She felt fifteen, alone and abandoned again.

Kelsey closed her eyes and pressed her fingers to her eyelids, stinging with fresh tears. God, she was going to cry. With great effort, she curled her fists and tamped down the panic welling inside her. "I practically lived in that car growing up."

Stu laid a hand on her shoulder. "You're tired and jet-lagged as hell. Your emotions are raw. Let Mitch figure out who's down there before you do anything."

Kelsey's head started to pound. She'd spent ten years trying to forget those last days with her mother. There were times when her workload had been so heavy that she'd manage to forget for a month or two. But as soon as she slowed down, the memories returned. How many times had she second-guessed herself? Had she said or done something to drive Donna away? "I know this all sounds crazy."

"It doesn't sound crazy," Mitch said. "But we need more facts."

"I know I am right." Kelsey shook her head. "It never once occurred to me that Donna was dead. She always said she was like a cockroach. Couldn't be killed."

Mitch reached for her shoulder to comfort her and then, as if thinking better of it, planted his hands on his narrow hips. "Don't borrow trouble."

Kelsey started toward the water. The ripples from their dive had vanished. "I need to go back down there. There has to be something that'll tell me what happened."

Mitch grabbed her arm. "You're not going back down there. You're too shaky."

"Look, I bailed Donna out of trouble too many times. I can't just leave her there." Old habits died hard. "I have to go."

Skepticism darkened his eyes. "I'll call a few friends in Roanoke County. When they get here, we'll dive again after my surface interval."

God, he didn't understand. She didn't *want* to go. She *had* to. "I'm going."

Steel glinted in his eyes. "I'll hog-tie you first."

"You wouldn't do that."

"Watch me."

"I didn't panic underwater," Kelsey said as evenly as she could. "I held it together."

Mitch unfastened his weight belt. "You were rattled. You're still rattled. Diving when you are upset is stupid. You know that."

He was right, but she *could* hold it together. "I'm an experienced diver. I can handle it."

Stu shifted his weight off his injured leg. "Kelsey, you can't go back down. Not now. Hell, even Mitch has got to take an hour-long surface interval before he dives again."

She threw up her hands. "Okay, I wait an hour."

"No," Mitch said.

Mitch's wet black hair was slicked back. His face was all hard planes and rawboned angles. Moving a mountain would be easier than changing his mind right now.

An unshakable weariness settled into her bones. "I'm not leaving until Donna is out of that car. I can't leave her there. *I just can't.*"

17

Mitch studied her face. For an instant, she imagined the hard lines around his mouth softened. "Like I said, I'll call over to the next county. They've got an underwater search and recovery team. They'll check it out, bring up the car if necessary."

Kelsey's hand trembled as she pushed the wet hair away from her face. "How long will it take?"

"I don't know. But you might as well go back to town with Stu. Get something to eat, rest. I promise I will call you when I know something."

"That's a great idea, Kelsey," Stu said. "I'll bet you haven't had a decent meal in days."

A week was more like it. "Okay, I get the not-diving part. I *might* be a liability underwater now. But I'm staying right here in this spot until that car is inspected."

Mitch glared at her, his hands on his hips. "You will be sitting here most of the day. There's nothing you can do to help the investigation."

She could be just as stubborn as he was. "I'll wait."

He looked at her as if she were a nut job. "You've waited ten years for news of your mother. What are a few more days?" Mitch said. "Go back to town. Be reasonable."

Hysterical laughter rose in her throat. "I haven't been reasonable since the day Donna walked out on me. Why should I start now?"

18

# Chapter 3

Six hours later, the hot sun had burned off the morning haze, leaving a crystal-clear sky. Kelsey had shrugged off her dive suit and pulled on jeans and a shirt over her bikini.

Time and distance had settled the panic inside her. But a dull, lingering ache had burrowed into her bones. Her throat remained tight with unshed tears.

On Mitch's orders, she stood away from the quarry's edge, far from the search and recovery crew that had assembled there two hours ago. The six-man team had arrived shortly after eleven in a blue van marked Recovery Team. Attached to the back of their truck was a trailer and skiff.

The team immediately set up their equipment and inspected their dive gear. The quiet quarry buzzed with activity as Mitch briefed the men. Each man clearly liked and respected Mitch.

Now the skiff sat anchored in the middle of the quarry. Two policemen in the boat kept looking over the side into the water. They were waiting for the three divers below to come up to the surface. One of the divers was Mitch.

Two cops stood twenty feet away from Kelsey and chatted easily about a drug bust. Once or twice, they glanced at her, as if to make sure she'd not moved closer to the water's edge.

Mitch's doing, she thought grimly. He didn't trust her not to suit up and dive. He was right to be worried. Any other time, she'd have known better not to attempt a dive. But today, reason took a backseat to emotion.

Kelsey pressed her fingers to her now throbbing forehead. She thought she'd gotten past all the old feelings of abandonment and worry. She hadn't. Ten years later and Donna still could turn her world upside down.

Stu limped toward her. He shifted the weight on his foot, as if it was really bothering him. "Don't worry. Mitch has everything under control."

Kelsey hadn't missed how naturally Mitch had fallen into the leadership role of this recovery operation. "You should sit down. Take some weight off that ankle."

"I will soon."

Kelsey wrapped her arms around her shoulders. "Donna always liked being the center of attention."

Stu smiled. "She'd be in her glory if she could see what was happening."

Just then, Mitch and the other divers surfaced in the center of the quarry. They climbed into the boat, removed their fins. The police officer sitting next to the engine started the motor. They rode to shore, their tanks glistening in the sunlight.

On shore, Mitch removed his mask and then shrugged off his tanks. He had Kelsey's camera hooked to his weight belt.

*Her camera.* She had forgotten all about dropping it. God, she *had* been rattled. That camera and its waterproof case had cost her a couple of grand.

The divers reached the shore and climbed out of the boat. Mitch said something to the other divers, then glanced up toward the shore at Kelsey.

Her insides tightened and for just an instant, she felt her knees buckle. "I don't like him."

"Who? Mitch?" Stu said. "Why?"

"Too bossy."

"You two did fight like cats and dogs when you worked in the shop."

"Yeah."

He scratched his head. "Never saw two people who couldn't agree on anything."

"I feel like I can't breathe when he's close." She shoved a shaky hand through her hair, now dried by the sun.

Mitch carried his tanks to his car, which he'd moved down the ramp closer to the quarry and the recovery team truck. He unzipped his scuba suit and peeled it off. Opening the front door of his Suburban, he pulled out a towel and dried his hands and face. He shrugged on an old T-shirt.

One arm leaning on the roof of the car, he rested a foot on the running board and reached inside for the radio mounted to the dash.

"The guy did just scramble a dive team in less than two hours," Stu said. "I don't know law enforcement, but I'd be willing to bet he pulled off a minor miracle."

She hated owing anyone, especially Mitch. "I know."

"You should do something nice for him."

"Like what, bake a pie?"

Stu chuckled. "How about saying thanks?"

Kelsey sighed. She was being a bitch. "How many times am I going to have to clean up one of Donna's messes?"

Stu put his hand on her shoulder. "I know she could be tough to deal with." He sighed. "I wish to hell Chris and I had investigated the wreck better. We spotted it at the end of our dive and didn't have the air to spend. We'd planned to come back the next day and push it over the ledge, but that damn tourist nearly ran me over and then Chris took off. If we'd been able to check the car out, I could have spared you all this."

"It's okay, Stu," she said managing a smile. He'd always tried to be there for her. "Sooner or later, I'd have found out."

21

The image of the skeleton lying on the front seat flashed in her mind. She felt like she did those first nights after Donna had left. Powerless.

"Mitch is headed this way," Stu said. "He doesn't look happy."

She straightened her shoulders. "Does he ever?"

Stu laughed. "He's got a wicked sense of humor, as a matter of fact. Throws a mean football spiral." His tone more serious, he added, "He's a good guy, Kelsey. You can trust him."

Her spine straightened. "I trust you, Stu. That's it."

His aviator glasses on, Mitch strode toward them. He walked with the swagger of a military man. She bet he still made his bed to regulation, corners tucked, blankets firm enough to bounce a quarter. The guy was definitely wrapped tight.

Mitch handed Kelsey her camera. Their fingers brushed and every muscle in her body constricted. Who was she kidding? She was the one wrapped tight.

"Thanks," she said her voice rusty. "Seems I owe you a lot."

"You don't owe me anything." His gaze lingered on her a beat too long and then shifted to Stu. "Can I talk to you for a minute?"

Stu glanced nervously at Kelsey. "Sure, Mitch."

"Wait a minute. What about me?" Kelsey said stepping forward. "I've a right to know what's going on down there."

Tension invaded Mitch's muscles. "It might be better if I talk to Stu first."

She could feel the hysteria building inside her. "You're not cutting me out of this one, *Sheriff*."

Mitch's shoulders stiffened. He obviously didn't like being told what to do. "All right. I just radioed the morgue. When the hearse arrives, we'll bring the body up."

Morgue. Hearse. The breath rushed from her chest. "It was Donna in the car, wasn't it?"

Mitch's face softened a fraction. "We don't know that, Kelsey."

"I do." A sick feeling settled in the pit of her stomach.

Stu laid his hand on her shoulder and said something to her, but she barely registered the words.

"We need to wait for forensics and the autopsy," Mitch said. And then, as if reading her thoughts, he added, "We'll have a confirmation soon enough."

*Soon.* "How soon is soon?"

"We've got to get the body to shore and then get it to the medical examiner. A few days. Be patient," Mitch said.

Patient. The irony of his words made her choke with rage. "I've been *patient* for ten damn years, Sheriff," she said.

The policemen stopped what they were doing and turned in her direction. Mitch took her anger in his stride.

The pained look in Stu's eyes reminded her of the social workers she'd dealt with all those times Donna had gotten arrested. "As soon as Mitch knows anything, he'll let you know."

Kelsey tightened her fingers into fists. She'd always imagined that Donna was out there somewhere alive and trying to turn her life around. In her dreams, her mother had realized that leaving her daughter had been the biggest mistake of her life. Donna wanted to return home to Kelsey, sober and loving. All the questions would have answers.

Her naiveté was almost laughable now. There were no answers. Only more questions. "Honey," Stu said, "you're exhausted. You need to rest."

Kelsey shoved aside her fatigue. "I'm not leaving."

"There's nothing you can do here," Mitch said.

She lifted her gaze to his mirrored shades. Her drawn expression stared back at her. "I always took care of Donna, even when I was real young. I'll wait until she is out of the water."

He was silent for a moment. "Fair enough."

She looked at Stu. "But I do want you to go back to town. Your leg must be throbbing by now."

Stu winced and she saw the strain in his face. He was hurting. "I'm not leaving you."

"She's right, Stu," Mitch said. "I'll have a policeman drive you back."

She handed Mitch her car keys. "Take my car."

Stu shook his head. "Thanks, you two, but I'm staying." His voice sounded shaky. He was only fifty-five, yet he looked seventy. This had all been a terrible strain on Stu. She reminded herself that he'd once loved Donna.

The tremor in his voice endangered Kelsey's hold on her composure. She didn't want to lose him, too. "I'm used to being alone. And I can't focus on Donna if I'm worried about you. Please, for me, go back to town and take care of yourself."

Stu stared at her an extra beat, then shoved out a sigh. "I'm not leaving you, Kelsey."

She laid her hand on his shoulder. His skin felt cold. "Please, Stu, go home and put your foot up."

He laid his hand over hers. "How will you get back?"

"I'll bring her," Mitch offered.

His rusty voice radiated authority. And she'd have argued with Mitch just for the sake of it, if not for the look of relief on Stu's face.

She managed one of her best smiles. "See, all taken care of."

A hint of a smile tugged the edges of Mitch's mouth. She hated accepting his help and he knew it. He called out to a policeman, "Jeff, can you take Stu back in Kelsey's car?"

The tall thin policeman nodded. "Be glad to."

Stu looked past her to Mitch. "You'll call me as soon as the body is up?"

"Promise," Mitch said.

"All right." Stu kissed Kelsey on the cheek. "Call me the minute you get back to town."

"That's the second promise you've asked me to make today," she said, trying to lighten the mood. "Making promises goes against my grain, but for you I'll make an exception."

Stu chuckled. "I'm old. I have a right to be greedy." Kelsey handed Jeff her keys and then helped Stu up the hill. His limp was more pronounced and his shoulders stooped.

Jeff slid behind the wheel and adjusted the seat back before starting the engine. He backed the car out of the parking area. Only when the car was out of sight did she turn and walk back toward Mitch. "Stu was always so full of life. I never figured he'd get old."

"He's got a lot of life left in him." The concern in Mitch's voice yanked at her heart. "Stu cares a lot about you."

His kindness threatened to shatter her shaky composure. "Do me a favor. Don't be nice to me. I don't trust *nice*. Whether it was Donna, the social workers or you, *nice* always signaled trouble—the rent wasn't paid, a stint in a foster home was coming or you didn't know what to do with an emotional, love-struck teenager."

His jaw tightened, released. "When's the last time you ate? Your skin is pasty and there are dark circles under your eyes."

She managed a shaky grin.

"There, that's more like it."

Shaking his head, he strode to his car and grabbed a thermos from behind the seat and a pack of Nabs from a cooler. He opened the red cap, poured coffee into a cup and handed it to her.

She stared into the steaming cup. "Thanks."

He tore open the packet of crackers. "Sorry, no cream and sugar."

Warmth from the hot cup seeped into her cold fingers. "Black's fine."

He handed her an orange square cracker. "I can still have one of my men drive you."

Kelsey sipped her coffee. Good. She ate the cracker.

To her relief, her stomach settled immediately. "I've been racking my brain trying to figure out who killed Donna."

Her comment caught him off guard. "Why would you think your mother was murdered?"

Kelsey fingered the cross that dangled from the chain around her neck. "Because of the company she kept. Petty thieves. Shoplifters. A few addicts."

25

Mitch shoved out a sigh. "When I talked to Stu earlier, he said she seemed on edge those last couple of days she was in town. What do you remember about those last days?"

"She kept talking about the money she was coming into. She said once she was done with her business here, we'd be set for life. No more traveling. A real home. I didn't pay any attention because Donna had said it all before."

Mitch shook his head. "Did she say where the money was coming from?"

"No. For once she was very quiet about her plans. She wasn't even drinking much those last couple of days. I could tell because her hands trembled when she lit her cigarettes."

Mitch stared at the quarry. "Stu talked about Donna from time to time. He said he always figured she'd end up a movie star or married to a rich man."

Her mouth curved in a half smile. "She had a talent for getting under a man's skin. Stu was in love with her. They dated pretty seriously in high school. He was the one person in town who kept up with Donna. And no matter how nasty she could be, she never had a bad thing to say about her to me."

"What happened with them?"

"She left Stu for a richer man."

"Your father?"

"Maybe. I don't know." She sipped her coffee.

"You don't know who your father is?" His words were clipped.

Donna had never told Kelsey who her father was, no matter how much she'd begged. Not knowing had fueled her dreams of finding her father who she hoped would one day find her and make everything better. One day never came. "Not all of us have the *Leave It to Beaver* life."

Her comment had a bite to it that he hadn't missed. "Children deserve a home." He spoke softly, but there was steel behind each word.

The image of a home—a real house with a front porch and

26

a yard—had been another one of her dreams when she'd been a child. She'd given up on fairy tales a long time ago.

Unsettled, she took a step away from him. Mitch Garrett was not going to let her feel sorry for herself. "So, do you moonlight with social services?"

His dark glasses tossed back her reflection, but she imagined his eyes had hardened. "Do you always have a smart answer for everything?"

She shrugged. "On my good days."

He muttered an oath. "You haven't changed a bit."

She shoved aside memories and regrets. "I'm not a naive eighteen-year-old anymore, Sheriff."

His broad shoulders stiffened. He looked as if he wanted to say something, but the words didn't come. Good to know she wasn't the only one who felt awkward.

The sound of car wheels crunching against gravel came from the road and tore his attention from her.

"That's the hearse," Mitch said, his voice brusque.

"You're not going to bring the car up?"

"Not for now. We're bringing the body up. I've got to go down to the quarry for a minute. Stay put. I want you where I can see you."

"I'm not going anywhere."

A large black car parked at the edge of the parking lot. Mitch left her to meet the driver. Once the stretcher and body bag were out of the car, the two men walked down to the edge of the water.

Mitch signaled the policeman in the skiff, who in turn radioed down to the divers as he drove the flat-bottomed boat to the quarry's shore. The driver took the bag from Mitch and drove back out to the middle of the quarry. A diver appeared from under the water and took the bag.

Mitch strode back toward her. Sunlight reflected on his aviator sunglasses. He stood next to her in silence.

27

She hugged her arms around her chest as she stared at all the police and rescue men.

The divers surfaced and gave the thumbs-up. A body bag rose to the surface. Water bubbles gurgled to the surface. The divers hooked the black bag to the side of the boat. It floated by the boat.

Kelsey's stomach tightened. She felt sick.

Mitch glanced at her. His frown deepened. "We'll stay back here while the men do their work."

"Okay."

He raised an eyebrow. "No argument?"

She couldn't even manage a weak smile. "Sorry, fresh out. Maybe tomorrow."

The boat's motor hummed as the skiff moved closer to shore. Minutes passed slowly.

Mitch yanked off his sunglasses. "You look like you're going to pass out."

She wanted to throw up. "I'm fine."

The boat skidded against the rocky shore. Two other officers took the body bag. A cop opened the zipper a fraction so that the water could drain. He met Mitch's gaze and nodded as if to confirm what they'd seen earlier.

None of this felt real.

Suddenly Kelsey broke into a full run toward the bag. She shouldered her way past the police and looked into the sack. A thick mossy smell drifted up as the water drained. In the bag was the skeleton.

Years of hoping and worrying exploded. Suddenly, her head started spinning. Her mother really hadn't abandoned her. Her mother had died.

Mitch laid his hand on her shoulder. Warmth and strength radiated into her. She remembered a time when his strong arms had wrapped around her body and, for a few precious hours, she had felt safe and secure.

His voice was low and soft next to her ear. "Let's get out of here."

28

# Chapter 4

Kelsey climbed into the front cab of Mitch's Suburban and shut the door. She soaked up the sun's warmth trapped in the leather seats. A chill shuddered through her body. She'd never been so cold before.

Mitch slid into the driver's seat beside her, put the keys in the ignition and started the car. Silent, he drove down the gravel drive toward the main road. The wooded landscape skidded by in a blur of green. When gravel met pavement, Mitch paused, checked for traffic and then turned left onto the highway. Billboards and vegetable stands dotted the roadside before giving way to gas stations and then strip malls as they neared town.

Grant's Forge was over one hundred and fifty years old. It had seen Civil War battles, the loss of the rail lines and in the 1970s, the flight of businesses to the outlying strip malls. By the early 1980s, the town's buildings were run-down and in danger of demolition. Then several prominent ladies in town took it upon themselves to revitalize the dying historic center. Timed with the Washington, D.C. real estate explosion, the crumbling buildings quickly found a second life as host to tiny shops and restaurants that catered to the busy urbanites looking for weekend getaways. The town was described as "an idyllic spot, a gold mine of history and amusements reminiscent of days gone by" in *Traveler* magazine.

To Kelsey, Grant's Forge conjured up memories she'd just as soon forget.

The sun glinted off the face of Mitch's gold wristwatch, drawing her gaze to his long fingers wrapped tightly around the steering wheel. She remembered those hands on her body. Memories.

There'd been a time when she'd shared so much with this man—her hopes, her dreams, her body—but now he was a stranger. And she'd never felt more alone and isolated.

Kelsey caught herself. Quiet moments like these gave her time to brood and were always her undoing. She usually went out of her way to fill the silence, often working seven days a week, ten hours a day.

"So how long have you been back in Grant's Forge?" she asked. A dumb question, but it was better than silence.

Mitch glanced at her, surprised she'd spoken. He relaxed a fraction, as if he, too, wasn't comfortable with the quiet. "Three years."

Her bracelets rattled as she brushed her hair off her face. "What brought you back?"

His expression remained stoic. "Dad had a bad heart attack. It really shook us all up. I decided my days of traveling were over. It was time to come home."

The Garretts had always been close. Many times, she'd envied them. The fact that Mitch was from a tight-knit family had been one of the things she'd once found attractive about him. "Stu said something in one of his letters about marriage." The idea that Mitch was married irritated.

"Alexandra didn't go for the small-town life."

*Alexandra.* Sounded rich, expensive, spoiled—the exact opposite of her. Everything she had today she'd gotten by sweating and scraping. "She left?" Kelsey hated the hopefulness in her voice.

"We divorced two years ago." Under his simply spoken words,

she sensed tension and anger. His parents' marriage was rock-solid and his divorce likely hadn't sat well with him.

"Sorry." She didn't feel all that *sorry* but didn't know what else to say.

Mitch turned right onto Main Street and headed into the historic district. "It happens."

He drove past all the fashionable row houses filled with high-end stores and a trendy coffee house.

"You can drop me at Yancey's Motel. I've got a room there." She'd not been able to bring herself to stay at her aunt's house. More bad memories.

"Let's stop by the Third Street Diner and get a bite to eat first."

Her stomach tightened at the thought of food. "Thanks, but I'll pass."

Sunlight glinted off his sunglasses as he shot her a quick look. "You need to eat."

He'd always been good at giving orders. "I'm a better judge of that than you."

"Doubtful."

"You're a pain in the ass, Garrett," Kelsey said. She folded her arms over her chest.

A grin tugged the edge of his mouth. "Glad to see I haven't lost my touch."

The Third Street Diner was at the edge of the historic district. A throwback to the 1950s, the diner hadn't been renovated like the other establishments. It stubbornly clung to the small-town way of life Grant's Forge had once enjoyed. The diner's bright chrome caught the afternoon light. The *R* in Third blinked slower and out of time with the rest of the blue and green neon letters.

"The Third Street Diner is the last place I want to eat. Every local in town will be there on Sunday afternoon." And none would be glad to see her. Not only had she missed her aunt's funeral, but her mother hadn't exactly ingratiated herself to others.

Mitch put the car in Park and shut off the engine. He pulled

31

off his sunglasses and met her gaze. "We'll get a booth in the back. You need to eat, Kelsey." The softness had crept back into his voice.

"Then take me by a convenience store and I'll get crackers and a soda."

He cocked an eyebrow. "You aren't afraid of a few old gossips, are you?"

The challenge in his voice had her lifting her chin. "No. But right now, I don't have the patience to deal with a bunch of yokels who want to remind me that I'm no good, like my mother."

His eyes hardened. "First one that does has to deal with me."

The strength in his voice soothed her nerves. She believed him. She sighed.

"I'll take that as a yes," he said getting out of the car.

As he moved around the front of the Suburban, she climbed out of the vehicle. Her legs felt wobbly and her stomach queasy. It had been a good twenty-four hours since she'd eaten a real meal. And the diner's pancakes were the best.

She closed the car door and glanced up at the diner as Mitch opened the glass front door and waited. She walked past him inside. The smell of burgers greeted her and for a moment, she was transported back in time. She'd eaten breakfast here a lot that last summer. Ruth had never been one for cooking and when Kelsey had started earning money at the scuba center she began treating herself to a hot meal here each day. She'd chosen the diner breakfast because it was cheap, plentiful and saw her through each day.

To their right was a glass display case. On top was the cash register and behind it stood Tammy Fox. Kelsey cringed and slid to Mitch's right, hoping the woman wouldn't notice her. They'd gone to high school together. Tammy had been a cheerleader and Kelsey the misfit foster kid. They'd locked horns from day one.

Tammy pulled down her stained white T-shirt over her pregnant belly as her gaze darted to the sheriff. "Hey, Mitch!"

"Tammy." He sounded formal.

"We saw the police trucks headed toward the quarry. Everything all right?" Tammy said.

Mitch tucked the arm of his sunglasses behind his T-shirt collar. "Nothing we can't handle."

Kelsey was grateful Mitch didn't go into the details. Soon everyone would know that Donna's body had been found and, when they did, she'd have no peace.

Maybe, just maybe, they would get to a table without a lot of conversation or trips down memory lane.

Tammy glanced around Mitch and spotted her. Damn. "Kelsey Warren, is that you?"

Normally, the diner would have been empty about three o'clock in the afternoon, but because it was Sunday, a lot of folks had lingered after lunch. The chatter grew quiet. Kelsey was very aware that everyone was staring.

Kelsey took a small step back and ran into Mitch's rock-hard body. He placed a hand on her shoulder. Her nerves stopped jumping so much.

Tammy's gaze skipped quickly to Mitch's hand and up to Kelsey's eyes. She grinned. Butter could have melted in Tammy's mouth. "I'd heard you were back in town but I didn't see you at the funeral yesterday. I must have missed you in the crowd."

Kelsey wasn't fooled. The cheerleader-turned-cashier was on the hunt. Her gaze slid to Tammy's full stomach. As tempted as she was to shoot back a smart-ass comment, she decided against it. "I was running late."

Mitch picked up a couple of menus. "We'll seat ourselves over in the corner."

"Sounds good. Go ahead," Tammy said.

Kelsey imagined Tammy was running through her list of friends, anxious to tell them that she'd seen Kelsey. Mona Winters would be first.

Mitch captured Kelsey's elbow and led her past the twenty-plus booths to the back. A flurry of whispered conversations ignited as they headed to the back of the diner.

Kelsey slid into the booth, her back to the door, and picked up a menu. No doubt she'd keep the gossips buzzing for months.

"They're not talking about you," Mitch said.

She peered over the edge of her menu and found him staring at her. She shifted on the vinyl bench seat. "You could have fooled me."

"It's the car Stu found. It's stirred quite a bit of questions these last couple of days."

"It's an abandoned car. Don't these people have lives or cable television?"

"The car might have gone unnoticed altogether if Stu hadn't been hit by a car night before last."

Kelsey leaned forward. "Stu was hit by a car? He told me it was a clumsy accident."

"He keeps downplaying it, saying it was a tourist or a teen in a rush."

Her heart beat faster. "What do you think?"

"It was dark and he didn't get any description. I was willing to believe he was right—until today."

"When we found Donna?"

He lowered his voice to correct her. "We found an unidentified body."

She didn't have the energy to argue. Soon his medical tests would prove her right. "So you think someone tried to kill Stu because he'd found the car."

"I don't know. Maybe it's just an odd coincidence. If he'd died, we'd never have found the car."

Tammy set two cups of coffee on the table. "Why, you two look cozy." She pulled a half-used order pad from her pocket and a pencil.

Kelsey sat straighter.

Mitch's jaw tightened.

Tammy seemed to savor the tension. "What can I get you two?"

Mitch nodded to Kelsey to go first. Her stomach rumbled. "Coffee is fine."

"Now don't tell me you are one of those anorexics, Kelsey," Tammy said. "You're pencil-thin."

Kelsey glanced up at Tammy's moon-shaped face. The former cheerleader's sharp cheekbones had long disappeared. She didn't have the energy to toss an insult her way. "No appetite."

"We'll have two number fours," Mitch said. He took Kelsey's menu and handed it to Tammy.

Tammy lingered an extra beat, as if hoping to hear or learn something. But when Mitch lifted a questioning gaze, she lost her nerve and left.

Kelsey sipped her coffee. It tasted bitter, the bottom of the pot.

"Can you tell me about the last time you saw your mother?" Mitch said.

She'd spent so much time trying to forget that day. Yet it took no effort to retrieve it. "It was ten years ago. I was fifteen. We'd been in town a couple of days. Like I said, Donna kept talking about a big score—more money than we could ever dream of. That last night I was watching TV, trying to stay out of Aunt Ruth's way—she didn't like having us in her house and didn't mind telling Donna that. Donna kept talking about the money she'd give Ruth if she just played along for a couple more days."

Mitch listened, his gaze boring into her.

Kelsey pushed her cup aside. "Anyway, it was past nine in the evening when Donna went out. She was wearing her favorite jeans and black leather vest—the outfit she always wore when she went barhopping. I figured she was going out for a drink. But she never came back."

"You never heard from her again?"

"No. But at first, I figured all her talk of money was just a ploy to buy time with Ruth for a few days. She often took off for days on end. I really thought she'd turn up. That went on for a few months."

Mitch frowned.

Tammy arrived with two plates full of pancakes, scrambled eggs, bacon and grits. She set them on the table. "Anything else?"

Her extra friendly tone was so sweet, Kelsey half expected her to pull up a chair, sit down and join their conversation. Mitch nixed that. "That's it." Tammy's smile wavered. She seemed disappointed to leave without the least bit of gossip. "Well, you just holler if you need me." She left.

"You're ruining her day," Kelsey said. "She'll have nothing to tell Mona and Nancy."

He looked surprised and then a faint smile tugged at the edge of his lips. His face softened and he looked all the more handsome. "I keep forgetting you went to high school here."

"Junior and senior year."

"What did you do after you left Grant's Forge?" His gaze was hooded and she desperately wanted to read his mind.

*You mean after you figured out I was a virgin and I ran for the hills?* "I just started traveling to wherever I could teach scuba." Her voice sounded so casual, but in truth an old sadness crept into her bones. In self-defense, she dropped her gaze to her plate. "I loved the diner's pancakes."

"I remember."

Warmth spread through her before she awkwardly picked up her fork. She took a bite of the pancakes and discovered they were as good as she remembered. She took a couple more bites, preferring to eat rather than to stroll down memory lane with Mitch.

He took the hint and dug into his meal. They were half finished when several folks shouted a greeting to a new arrival. Kelsey looked up over her shoulder. She saw a tall, silver-haired man in his mid-fifties wearing khakis and a white Polo shirt stroll into the diner. She'd never met the man, but knew him instantly.

Boyd Randall. He and his wife Sylvia were local royalty. They were worth more money than Midas and last night, when she couldn't sleep, she'd read in the paper that Boyd had decided to run for the U.S. Senate next year.

Boyd's quick, bright smile flashed as he passed several booths shaking hands and pausing to chat. However, it was quickly clear that he'd come to see Mitch. He strolled over to their booth, pulled up a chair and sat down. He glanced down at Kelsey. His hundred-watt smile vanished. "Kelsey Warren."

Kelsey shifted in her seat, annoyed at his tone. He spoke her name as if it left a bitter taste in his mouth. Normally, she wasn't so sensitive about slights. But she'd been a raw nerve since she'd arrived at Grant's Forge. "Mr. Randall."

Boyd shifted his gaze to Mitch, completely dismissing her. "Miss Warren, would you excuse us? I got some things to say to the sheriff."

Her body tensed.

Mitch shook his head. "No reason for Kelsey to leave."

Boyd's eyes narrowed. "What I got to say is private."

"If you want to schedule an appointment, I'll be happy to meet with you in private. Right now, we're having a meal."

A muscle in Boyd's jaw jumped. "I hear they found a body in the quarry."

Mitch's expression didn't reveal the first hint of emotion. He set his fork down. "Rumors fly fast."

"I got friends in high places. When the sheriff in my town calls for a recovery team, it sends up red flags and I get a call. What's going on?"

"We have found a body," Mitch said. He seemed to gauge each word very carefully. "But we have no idea who it is. The body is on its way to the state coroner's office."

"Any thoughts? Theories?"

"None," Mitch said.

"I have a theory," Kelsey said.

Boyd shifted his gaze to Kelsey. It didn't take higher math to know he wanted her out of town. "This should be rich."

Kelsey didn't blink. "I believe the body is my mother."

Boyd's vivid blue eyes didn't show a hint of shock.

"Is that true, Sheriff?"

Annoyance radiated from Mitch's body. "We don't know anything yet."

Boyd leaned closer. Powerful expensive aftershave drifted around them. "Then why does Miss Warren believe the body is her mother?"

"Theories don't mean anything until we have evidence," Mitch said tightly.

"I am right," Kelsey said.

Mitch gritted his teeth and shook his head. "Again, we have no evidence."

Boyd drummed his manicured fingers on the marbled table. "Evidence or not, I want to be kept up to date on every detail of this case. When you have identification, I want a call."

Mitch's jaw tightened. He clearly didn't like Boyd's tone. "I will release information to the public when it's appropriate."

Boyd's eyes narrowed. "You've got a reelection campaign coming up, Mitch. An unsolved murder could be a problem for you."

"No one has said a thing about murder," Mitch said.

"Come on, this is Donna Warren we're talking about," Boyd said. "Most of the people in town hated her enough to kill her."

Kelsey flinched. He was right, but hearing the words hurt.

Mitch looked ready to explode.

Boyd's electric smile returned as if he knew he'd gotten under Mitch's skin. "Don't screw things up with this investigation. And you'd be wise not to mess with *her* kind. Her mother was trash and I'd bet my last dollar she is, too."

Mitch stood so abruptly the plates on the table rattled.

Boyd took a step back.

Kelsey's insides tightened. "Speaking from past experience, Boyd?" she said.

Boyd's lips flattened into a thin line as he glared at her. *Bull's-eye.* "Do us all a favor, Miss Warren, and get out of town." He stalked off.

She tossed her napkin on the table and muttered an oath.

Mitch sat back in his seat. "Looks like I'm not the only one with a talent for getting under your skin."

# Chapter 5

Kelsey shrugged, forcing herself to breathe deeply and relax. She reminded herself that she'd met Mitch two years after Donna had left. She was grateful he'd not been in town to witness that terrible time in her life.

"Boyd and I crossed paths when I first came back to town," she said. "I'd just started working at the scuba center when he decided to take up the sport. For a few months, he was in and out of the shop a lot. He was always asking me questions about Donna. I never had any answers to give and finally he stopped coming by the shop. Frankly, he gives me the creeps."

Mitch sighed. "Why did he care about Donna?"

"Honestly, I wouldn't be surprised if they had a thing at one time. She did get around."

She dropped her gaze and stared at the speckled tabletop. Why couldn't she have had a normal mother who baked cookies and drove her to soccer practice? "You ready to leave?" Mitch said softly.

"Yeah, I've had just about all the fun I can take."

Mitch paid the bill and escorted Kelsey to his Suburban. As she settled into the sun-warmed seat, the energy suddenly drained from her body. She could barely lift an arm.

Mitch's aviators glinted in the sun as he slid into the driver's side, started the car, and pulled out into traffic. "I'll take you to Yancey's. You look like you could sleep."

"Should you check in with your office and see if they've found out anything?"

He shook his head. "There won't be anything this early. As much as I'd like to rush the autopsy for you, these things just take time." He stopped at a red light and put on his right blinker.

"Could you drop me off at Ruth's?" She could hardly believe she'd asked the question.

"What for?"

"Who knows? I might stumble across something that belonged to Donna that could tell me more about her last few days in town."

He frowned. "You're better off at Yancey's Motel getting rest. Clues can wait until tomorrow, Nancy Drew."

She lifted an eyebrow. "You keep mistaking me for a reasonable person, Mitch. I'm not."

"Go to the motel."

She sat a little straighter. "Look, I don't have the energy to argue. If you drop me at the hotel, I'll just walk to Ruth's. So do me a favor and save me the five-block walk."

He glanced at her, his firm jaw set like granite. The light turned green but instead of turning right, he glanced in the rearview mirror to check traffic and, when it was clear, turned left toward Ruth's.

He drove down Second Street past the older buildings toward the town's oldest residential neighborhood. Thick oaks lined the curbed streets flanked by neat lawns and large blooming pink, white and red azaleas.

"So where did you and your mother live while you were away from Grant's Forge?"

"We traveled a lot. We never stayed in one place for more than a year."

"What'd she do for a living?" When they'd worked together,

he'd asked about her mother, but she'd always dodged the questions.

Kelsey shoved her hand through her hair. "Whatever suited her. There was a time when she wanted to be an actress. I was real little then. So we moved to L.A. But she spent most of her time waiting tables, so we headed north to Seattle. She worked in a bakery and for a while we had all the day-old cookies and bread we could eat. I liked the school there, but the rain depressed Donna. She got into drugs and I ended up in foster care for a while."

Mitch tightened his hands on the steering wheel, but he said nothing. People often got very uncomfortable when she talked about her childhood. If they'd grown up in a happy home, her stories made them feel guilty. If they'd had a bad time, she was a tangible reminder. So she'd stopped talking about herself.

"Anyway, to make a long story short, we jumped around the country until we landed here when I was fifteen."

"Your mother ever make any enemies?"

"Lots. She had a knack for pissing people off." He turned onto Mulberry Street—her aunt's street—and she found herself tensing. The trees were a little larger, but other than that, the row houses were exactly as she remembered.

Mitch pulled up in front of Ruth's house without having to ask the address. His familiarity with her life irked her.

She reached for her duffel bag and pulled out her camera. She popped a disk from the camera. "These are the pictures of the car. They might help you." She was grateful to get rid of the images.

Mitch tucked the disk in his pocket. "I'll get this copied and returned."

She closed up her camera and replaced it in the duffel. "Great. Thanks for the lift."

He shut off the engine. "Do you have a key?"

"Ruth always hid one under the flowerpot on the front porch. My guess is that it's still there." She opened her door and, to her surprise, he also got out. "I can take it from here."

He didn't miss a step. "Just making sure you get in all right."

His overprotectiveness should have irritated her, but she found it oddly comforting. There was something rock-solid about Mitch that comforted her more than words ever could.

Fishing for, but not coming up with, a smart remark, she settled on silence and walked up the cracked sidewalk up to the covered front porch that stretched the length of the house. The black front door had been freshly painted and the brass mail slot in the center of the door and kick plate glistened in the afternoon sun. A lime-green metal glider sat to her right, and to her left a white wicker chair and a large clay pot that held wilted red geraniums.

She tipped back the geranium pot and easily found the front door key. "Ruth didn't change a thing." "Older folks don't usually."

She slid the key into the lock. "She's been old forever."

"Eighty-seven when she died." The news surprised Kelsey. She'd never known how old Ruth was. The woman would have been in her mid-seventies when she'd taken Kelsey in. Few women of that age would have taken on a surly teen, and Kelsey couldn't help but admire her aunt.

She turned the key and opened the door. A week's worth of mail had piled in the darkened entryway, forcing Kelsey to kneel down and pick it up. As always, the house smelled of overcooked green beans and bacon grease. Her stomach soured.

As she stood with the mail, Mitch switched on the light. Two of the three bulbs in the ceiling light fixture were blown and the remaining one cast eerie shadows down the long center hallway. Dust floated in the air and coated the side table. A smudged mirror hung to her right. Floor-to-ceiling newspapers and shoe boxes lined the hallway.

Mitch yanked off his glasses. He scanned the clutter and dust. "What happened here?"

"Home sweet home."

"The place had always looked like this?"

Kelsey remembered the first time she'd seen the inside of the house. She'd half expected Herman and Lily Munster to walk down the stairs. "Yep."

"I had no idea."

"Most people didn't. Ruth was always good about keeping the exterior and the front hallway clean. The other rooms must really be full if her mess was moved out here."

"Damn."

She shrugged. "Look on the bright side. If there was ever any clue about Donna, Ruth has it tucked away somewhere. It's just a matter of finding it."

Mitch followed Kelsey down the hallway through the maze of rooms filled with more papers and boxes. As he stepped over crate after crate, he had a new appreciation for Kelsey. She'd not only survived Donna but this insanity as well. And to top it off, she'd gotten out and made something of herself. He stared at the long dining room table piled high with rows and rows of mismatched socks. "I can't believe you lived in this mess."

"Two glorious years." She wandered toward the hallway and the carpeted center staircase. "She let me keep my room clean."

He followed Kelsey up the stairs to a door at the end of the hallway. She pushed it open and stepped inside.

The room was unlike any other in the house. It was very neat. The double bed and dresser and mirror were simply made and not very expensive, but other than a coating of dust they were clean. Teen posters, along with snapshots taken by Kelsey, still covered the walls. The photos were of cats, dogs, birds and a circus elephant. No people, he noted wryly. The bedspread and curtains were a deep purple and covered with large yellow flowers.

Kelsey opened the curtains and let the sunlight stream in, catching the blond streaks in her hair. His gut tightened as he looked at her and he wanted to pull her into his arms, protect her and, yes, see if she still felt as soft as she once had.

"When I first moved in, it took me a solid week of cleaning to clear out this room. It drove Ruth nuts and she wouldn't let me throw anything out. I had to move everything to the attic, but I insisted on an organized room. Since I was a little kid, I've always been a stickler for organization and neatness."

A clean room was about the only thing she could control in her life. He remembered how precisely her dive equipment had been arranged on the tarp by the quarry. "Do you really think you can find anything about Donna in this place?"

"If anything, I am persistent. And if the medical examiner takes as long as you say he will, it will give me something to do."

"I've got a truck you can borrow."

"How about a forklift?"

He laughed. "It could be arranged."

"I might take you up on it." She set her cloth sack purse on the bed and headed downstairs.

"You're not really going to stay here, are you?" He hated the idea of leaving her here.

She shrugged. "I might as well. I'll save money and have more time to work on this place."

He studied her a moment. "All right. I'll bring your car by in a few hours. At least you'll be able to get around town."

"Thanks."

A mouse scurried behind a stack of papers. Mitch hesitated a moment. "Take care."

She followed him to the front door. The debris in the house seemed to press in around him like a wraith. When he jerked the front door open, sunlight flooded into the dreariness.

He got in his car. As he drove down the street, he glanced in his rearview mirror at her standing and watching him leave. Sadness seemed to settle on her slumped shoulders. There'd been a time when he'd made her so happy. And now, like everything else in this town, he only conjured up sad memories.

Mitch expected the protective urge he felt for Kelsey to fade, but he couldn't shake the image of her standing in the doorway. He didn't like leaving her there one bit. The damn place gave him the creeps.

Instead of heading north toward his home in the hills outside of town, he turned south toward the office. He wanted to poke through the department's old files and see if there was anything on Donna Warren.

He parked in front of the one-story square building. Unlike the buildings in the historic district, the police department was housed in a simple modular structure. It had no character and few windows. The lack of windows bothered him. Often he'd said he'd take a pay cut for a large window he could open and close.

Mitch walked up the concrete sidewalk to the double glass doors. Mabel Riley sat at the dispatcher's desk. She'd worked at the station for a good twenty years and she knew everyone in town. She'd tied her gray hair back and wore her customary white collared shirt and khaki pants. She wasn't a cop, but she'd always liked the idea of having a uniform.

"There's no word on the body yet," she said, reading his mind. "It's on its way to Richmond."

"I didn't figure there'd be news. I just thought I'd look in some of the old files and see what I could find."

"So you think the body is Donna?"

Mitch lifted a brow. "Do you know everything that goes on in this town?"

"And then some." Her voice rumbled like raw whiskey. "So is the body Donna Warren?"

He moved to the front desk and hitched his hip up on the edge. "I don't know. Kelsey Warren sure thinks it is."

"Why?"

"A bracelet found on the body. She said she gave it to Donna for Mother's Day."

Mabel shrugged. "Donna could have hocked it. She'd have sold anything for money."

"You knew Donna?"

"Went to high school with her. We weren't friends but knew of each other."

"So she as wild as they say?"

"Oh, yeah. She discovered men when she was fifteen and never looked back. Ran through them like tissue paper. She was a real user."

The bitterness in Mabel's voice surprised him. "How did Kelsey figure into all this?"

"I don't know much about the kid. I'd joined the army right after high school and by the time I got back, Donna had left town."

"Any files on Donna?"

"I'm a step ahead of you there, boss." A smug smile curved the edges of her thin lips as she pulled out a stack of yellowed files. "I went down to the records department and pulled what I could find on Donna. There's not much. Mostly petty stuff."

Mitch accepted the files. "Mabel, you scare me sometimes."

She grinned. "Part of the job, baby."

Mitch retreated down the hallway to his office in the back. The room was simply furnished with a large desk, a computer and file cabinets. There was a small round conference table, covered with piles of files, across the room. He liked keeping the active files in sight so they weren't forgotten. But after seeing Ruth's house, he resolved to clean it up when he got the chance.

Though he'd held the office for two years, he'd not gotten around to hanging pictures on the walls. He did have a browning plant his mother had given him and a picture on the wall of the Blue Ridge Mountains that had come with the office.

He sat down in the rolling chair and slid under his desk. He flipped open the first picture.

Stapled on the left inside flap was a mug shot of Donna Warren taken when she was about eighteen. For a moment, Mitch stared at her, dumbstruck. At first glance, she was the spitting image of Kelsey. Substitute Donna's Farrah Fawcett hairdo for Kelsey's sleek straight cut and they could have been twins.

But the more he stared at the picture, the more he saw differences. Even as young as she had been, Donna possessed a hardness in her eyes. And her eyes were brown, not the deep rich blue of Kelsey's.

He set the picture down and scanned the record. Mabel was right. There wasn't much here. Donna had gotten in trouble when she was fourteen for stealing jewelry from the department store. A year later, Ruth filed charges against Donna for stealing money from her, but she later dropped the charges. A couple of drunk and disorderly charges followed and then nothing. Donna was trouble, but there was nothing here in the records to hint at a murder motive.

Mitch leaned back in his chair. Donna would have been about twenty when Kelsey was born. He searched his memory back to the days he and Kelsey had worked together at the scuba center.

He remembered the first time he'd really noticed Kelsey. It had been his first day working in the scuba shop one hot June morning. She'd been working behind the counter, laughing at a joke of Stu's. Her laughter had rung in his head like church bells. So he'd bought her a soda that afternoon and invited her to sit out back with him. She'd blushed deeply and hesitated before she'd agreed. She'd worn a blue tank top, white shorts and flip-flops. He'd wanted to kiss her.

Instead, he'd asked her about herself. She'd dodged most of his questions. But she had told him that she'd been born in Richmond. *Richmond.* He wished now he'd had enough sense to press for answers. He wasn't sure what he could have done for her, but he should have shown more interest.

Mitch shook off the memory.

He sent a telex to the Richmond City Police Department. He briefed them on the body that had been found and requested information on Donna Warren. Kelsey had said they'd lived in

48

Los Angeles and Seattle so he telexed the police departments out there as well.

He didn't know where the Donna Warren trail would lead, but he was willing to follow it for Kelsey's sake. He owed her that much.

Mitch checked his watch. He'd left Kelsey over an hour ago.

He could get her car from the Yancey Motel and deliver it to her. Maybe on the way, he could pick up some Chinese food. She'd not eaten much at the diner and had to be hungry. "Or you could leave her the hell alone," he muttered to himself.

He closed his eyes and pinched the bridge of his nose. His head throbbed.

What the devil was he thinking? He and Kelsey were oil and water. He was rooted to Grant's Forge and she'd be gone as soon as the investigation was complete.

They had no future together and, after seeing Ruth's house, he guessed she had more issues than a politician. Damn.

He should leave well enough alone.

He should.

But he didn't.

"Mabel, get Harris on the phone. I need a lift over to the Yancey Motel."

# Chapter 6

Kelsey heard the car pull into Ruth's driveway at half past seven. She let loose the garbage bag she'd been filling with old newspapers and walked to the front window to peer out. To her surprise, it was Mitch driving her car. Behind him in his car was a Grant's Forge cop and behind him another cop in a patrol car. She'd never expected Mitch to return so soon. His promptness was oddly touching.

Kelsey set the bag aside and walked out onto the front porch. Crickets hummed and moths darted around the front porch light. Mitch waved to the other officer, who climbed into the patrol car and drove off, and then strode toward the front porch. Carrying a large brown paper bag, he walked with the grace of a predator confident in his strength and skills. Her body tingled at the sight of him and she found herself wishing she'd brushed her hair.

"You got yourself a regular parade there, Sheriff," she said. Sarcasm seemed her best defense now.

Even white teeth flashed. "All I need is a whistle and a baton and I'll be all set."

She laughed. She could fall for this man very easily—again—and the idea frightened her. Why couldn't Mitch be thirty pounds overweight, balding, with a wife and three kids?

The cop climbed out of Mitch's car and into the one behind it. The officer behind the wheel tooted his horn and drove off. Mitch waved goodbye.

"So what's in the bag?" Her voice sounded a bit hoarse.

He paused at the bottom of the front porch, planting his foot on the second step. "Dinner. Seeing as lunch got nixed, I figured you were hungry."

The rich smells of ginger and chicken drifted from the bag. And on cue, her stomach grumbled.

She pressed her hand to her flat belly and despite her best efforts blushed with embarrassment.

"I see I'm just in time," he said.

"I appreciate the housecall, but I've got a lot of work to do in this place."

"A half-hour won't make a difference with this place." He stared up at the house. His distaste for it was clear. "I still can't get over this place. From the outside, it looks to be in mint condition."

"Ruth was always concerned about appearances. She didn't want the neighbors talking ill of her."

He shook his head. "It's a nice night. Let's eat outside."

"Thanks but—"

"No buts." He sat down on the porch, staking his claim, and started to unpack an assortment of white takeout boxes. He also produced two cups full of hot tea. He held out a plastic fork to her. "I didn't know what you liked, so I got a little of everything."

He'd slept with her—taken her virginity—and he didn't know what kind of Chinese food she liked. The irony irritated her and seemed all the more reason to tell him to shove off.

However, Mitch Garrett wasn't going anywhere. She could push the matter, but the truth was she was hungry. She took the fork and sat down on the step.

The evening air was soft and the sky was filled with hundreds of stars. She inhaled, grateful not to smell any dust.

51

She chose the box filled with stir-fried vegetables and dug in. It tasted good.

Mitch chose the beef dish. "So you uncovered anything yet?"

"I got my room cleaned up. Sheets changed, dusted. Now, I'm working my way through the newspapers. She has papers that go back thirty years."

He poked around the vegetables, stabbed a piece of beef and ate it. "I've got a couple of nephews, they're fourteen. Mouthy, but hardworking. I'll send them over tomorrow."

"That's very kind, but no thanks." Her debt to him was mounting too fast as it was. "Why not?"

"I'm not good at accepting help, if you hadn't noticed."

"I noticed." He rooted through the white box for more beef. "What's wrong with taking a little help?" "Strings. Help always comes with strings?" His jaw tightened slightly. "No strings, Kelsey. Just being neighborly."

"No easing any old guilt?" There, it was out.

"No."

The curt response confirmed her suspicions. "You do feel guilty."

"We were young."

She set down her box, her appetite suddenly gone. "But you believe you should have known better. Good and perfect Mitch Garrett slept with a troubled, teenaged virgin, broke her heart and it still eats at him." She heard the bitterness in her voice and it made her even madder.

"Kelsey," he said lowering his voice, "if I had known, I never would have slept with you."

She hated pity more than debt. "You just thought I knew the ropes." She shrugged, hoping he didn't notice the trembling in her hands. "Why shouldn't you? Like mother, like daughter, right?"

"I misjudged you."

"It was a long time ago." So why did the pain still linger?

He met her gaze and, almost against her will, held it. "We should talk about it."

52

"Look, it's been a real long day." As she stood, a dull ache began to pound in the back of her head. At the rate she was going, she'd have a full-blown migraine soon. "I'm tired. Thanks for dinner."

She didn't dare look at him as she walked inside the house and closed the massive front door. For a moment, her knees wobbled and she couldn't walk. She leaned against the door and closed her eyes. Tears spilled down her cheeks.

She heard Mitch pack up. His purposeful steps thudded on the front porch toward the door. He rang the bell. "Kelsey, let me in."

Every muscle in her body tensed. She didn't move, holding her breath until she heard him mutter an oath, turn and leave.

Kelsey exhaled. As much as she'd wanted to find her mother these last ten years, she prayed now that the body in the quarry wasn't Donna. Not knowing what had happened to Donna had been painful, but facing the past was excruciating.

Maybe Mitch and everyone else were right. Maybe the body didn't belong to Donna. She was the consummate survivor. A cockroach.

Late Monday afternoon, Mitch got the preliminary report back from the pathologist. The body was that of a woman in her early forties who was about five feet seven inches tall. The victim had endured several fractures, one on her face, one on her wrist and another on her ring finger on her right hand. The fractures had happened over the years and had healed with varying degrees of success. The victim hadn't had access to good medical care. The victim, judging by tooth decay, had been an addict.

Though no positive ID could be made until Donna's dental records had been examined, the evidence indicated that the body was Donna Warren.

There was another bit of information the autopsy had revealed. The victim had been murdered. According to the report, the victim had sustained a gunshot wound to the chest. The buckshot had shattered the left ribcage, most likely tearing directly into the heart muscle. She'd died instantly.

The fact that he now officially had a murder on his hands changed everything. He'd have to get the underwater crews back. The quarry and the woods around the upper lip of the quarry would have to be searched for evidence. Time had probably eradicated most of the evidence, but the search would occur nonetheless.

Mitch leaned back in his office chair. His first thought was of Kelsey. This information wouldn't sit well with her. After last night, his sloppy reminder of their past had shaken her fragile hold on serenity. He had wanted to clear the air but had only managed to muck things up more.

His phone buzzed and a green light blinked as Mabel's voice shot through the phone. "Mitch?"

"Yep?"

"The pathologist is on line one."

"Thanks."

Mitch's hand hovered over the black phone. He snatched it up. "Dave."

"Hey, Mitch." Dr. Dave Wilder had been a pathologist with the state for almost thirty years. He saw mostly accidents, but had handled hundreds of murders.

"What you got for me?"

"The body is definitely Donna Warren. I just reviewed the dental records. Granted, the victim's teeth were badly damaged, but I had a set of X-rays from a checkup Donna had had about twenty-seven years ago. They show a distinct overbite, two cavities on the back left molar and a chip on the front left incisor."

His first thought was for Kelsey. "Any other signs of trauma?"

"No skeletal signs. I can tell you that she was shot at close range. Less than five feet, maybe."

"Someone she knew." He didn't realize he'd spoken out loud.

Dave chuckled. "That's for you to find out. I've got more tests to run and if I come up with anything unexpected, I'll give you a call."

"Thanks, Dave." Mitch hung up the phone. He rose and walked to the small window. The sky was crystal blue.

There was a knock at his door. He turned to see Mabel standing just inside his office, her yellow pad in hand. "Mitch?"

"Yeah?"

"Patrol just radioed in. They've found a car on the side of I-81."

"Okay, why do they need my input?"

"The car belongs to a Chris Hensel."

"Stu's partner?"

"Yeah."

Mitch got a sick feeling in the pit of his stomach. "Any sign of Chris?"

"No. No signs of struggle. Just the car, parked on the side of the road as if it belonged there."

"Mabel, tell the officers to keep this quiet. I don't want a lot of people traipsing around there. I've got enough thrill-seekers trying to get onto the quarry land."

"So what should they do?"

"Have them conduct a thorough search of the area. I want to make damn sure Chris isn't nearby. Tell them to treat it like a crime scene. Gloves, evidence kit, the works. And call the state prison and see if they can lend a team with bloodhounds."

"Will do."

The front door to the station house banged open and closed, rattling the glass entry wall. Irritated, Mitch stepped out of his office, loaded for bear.

Standing in the entryway was Boyd Randall. He wore khakis, a bright yellow shirt and golf shoes. The shoes' spikes clicked across the floor as he marched toward Mitch. "Any word on the body?"

Mitch turned to Mabel. "Go ahead and radio patrol."

"Consider it done," she said.

Mitch motioned his hand toward his office. "In my office."

Boyd marched inside and took a seat in front of Mitch's desk.

55

He crossed his leg over the other and tapped his knee. "Any updates on that body?"

Mitch closed the door. "All evidence suggests that the body is Donna."

Tension tightened his face. "Have you run DNA?"

He sat behind his desk. "It'll be a couple of weeks on that, but the dental records were positive."

Boyd sighed. "The last damn thing I need is a murder. It's not going to look good."

Mitch leaned forward. "Why the interest?"

"Let's just say an investigation into Donna Warren's life would not be the best thing for me."

"Why not?"

He hesitated, as if gauging each word very carefully. "Donna and I had a thing once."

"A thing?"

"We were lovers. It was a very long time ago."

"Before you married Mrs. Randall?"

"No. We'd been married about two years when I met Donna. Things weren't good with Sylvia, and Donna was available."

"You're not the first politician to have an affair."

Boyd fisted his fingers. "It was my first and only slip. It was very painful for Sylvia and it took a lot of work to rebuild the trust I had with her."

For some reason, Mitch believed that Boyd was genuinely concerned about his wife's feelings.

"I just don't want old business polluting what we have. She's not been well lately and she doesn't need this."

Boyd seemed earnest. But that didn't mean squat. "I'm not sure what you want me to do," Mitch said.

"Wrap this up as quickly and quietly as you can."

"I'm not sure if I can guarantee that. I don't know what I'm going to find when I start digging."

"You're going to find that Donna was a cold-hearted bitch who

56

used men like Kleenex. She had a dozen lovers in town and likely one of them got tired of paying her to be quiet."

The bitterness in Boyd's voice caught Mitch by surprise. "Sounds like you're talking about yourself."

He shook his head. "Like I said, I cut things off with Donna years ago. I didn't even know she'd returned to Grant's Forge that last time until I saw that kid of hers working in the scuba shop. What's her name?"

"Kelsey."

"Right." He shook his head. "The kid was all mouth in those days. Seems her mother had just taken off and left her with Ruth."

"We know now she didn't just take off. She'd been murdered."

"I sure didn't know that at the time."

No, but you were worried that Donna had returned to town. "Is there anything else you can tell me about Donna? You might know something that could lead me to her killer."

"Not much. She talked of moving to L.A. and being a star. She was always like that—plans bigger than her pocketbook. Once she took off for L.A., I never saw her again. That was twenty-plus years ago."

"Right." Mitch stood.

"Look, I don't want Sylvia hurt. She's a good woman and she deserves better than this."

Until Mitch had more evidence, there wasn't much more he and Boyd had to say to one another. But he sensed they'd chat again. "Thanks for stopping by. If you think of anything else about Donna, you will tell me?"

Boyd rose. He smoothed a thick lock of white hair off his face. "I sure will."

Mitch waited until Boyd left before he grabbed his hat. He was anxious to talk to Kelsey, but knew he needed to check out Chris's car first. "Mabel, I'm headed up I-81 and then over to Ruth Warren's house. I won't be back today." Whatever hopes he'd had of making an early evening of it were long gone.

Mitch spotted the patrol car and the blue Toyota Corolla parked on the side of I-81 South. He slowed and pulled over to the side, put his car in Park and shut off the engine. A cool breeze greeted him as he climbed out of the car and put on his hat.

Deputy Leonard Jackson, who'd been waiting for him in his car, got out. Jackson was a tall, lanky man with a thick mop of black hair. In his mid-twenties, he'd been with the town police force for six months. Jackson touched the brim of his hat. "Sheriff."

The gravel on the side of the road crunched under Mitch's boots. "What do you have for me?"

"It's Chris Hensel's car. I found it about an hour ago. I checked out the car—it was locked. There is no sign of Chris."

Mitch reached in his pocket and pulled out a set of keys. "I swung by the dive shop and picked up a spare set of Chris's keys from Stu."

"I'm surprised Stu didn't come."

Mitch inspected the car's black interior as he walked toward the back of the car. Other than several fast-food bags and cups, the car looked clean. "I didn't want him here. I promised I'd call if there was any trouble."

"Let's hope we don't find a body in this car."

Mitch shoved the key into the trunk lock. "Yeah." Chris had lived in Grant's Forge for at least ten years. He'd never been in any trouble that Mitch was aware of and was well liked in the community.

He turned the lock and the trunk opened. The trunk contained fins, a wet suit, a regulator, a beat-up brown cloth suitcase and a cooler filled with diet sodas. But there was no sign of Chris.

Jackson expelled a breath.

Mitch did, too. "Where the devil is Chris?" He moved to the driver's side and got in. He turned the key in the ignition and it started right up. The gas tank was full.

Mitch checked the glove box. Nothing out of the ordinary. He looked under the seats. Nothing.

"I've got a couple more men headed your way, Dieteck and Abley. When they get here, we can start searching the woods."

"Doesn't make any sense," Jackson said.

"No, it doesn't." Chris did have a history of heart trouble, so it was possible he could have run into trouble, and that a motorist had helped him. "Radio Mabel and have her check the area hospitals."

Just then, another patrol car pulled up and Dieteck and Abley got out. They only had a couple of hours of daylight left, but Mitch decided they needed to make the best of it. After radioing Mabel, the four men fanned out and started checking the woods.

It was four o'clock in the afternoon when Kelsey's front doorbell rang. She'd spent the better part of the day working her way through the downstairs hallway, throwing out piles of newspapers, decade-old piles of junk mail and all the other clutter she could find in the front hallway. The process was painstaking. Though she'd have loved to chuck all the junk, she felt as if she needed to check each and every bit, fearing if she didn't, she'd miss a clue about her mother.

Kelsey opened the door and standing on the front porch were two teenaged boys. Tall, slim with dark hair, they shared Mitch's deep blue eyes and square jaw. In many ways, they reminded her of the Mitch she'd known ten years ago.

"Hey," she said, recovering.

The boys stared at her for a moment, neither speaking as they took in the sight of her cut-offs, cropped white T-shirt streaked with newspaper print and her blond hair tied back with a bandana.

The older of the two was the first to recover. "Uncle Mitch sent us," he said. "My name is Rick and this is my younger brother Jeff. Mitch said you might need some bags hauled away."

She'd forgotten Mitch had said he'd send over his nephews. "Hi, I'm Kelsey."

Jeff grinned. "We'd have been here sooner, but school isn't out yet for the summer. Nine days to go until freedom." He looked as if he'd recently tried to shave his face. By the looks of it, he'd only managed to nick up his smooth skin. "We are here to help."

She couldn't help but smile. At Jeff's age, the last school days before summer vacation had flown by. She liked school and hated being home with Ruth all day. "You sure you want to spend a spring afternoon hauling dusty papers?"

Rick nodded. "Mitch said whatever you needed hauled away, we were to do it."

Mitch had remembered her and she was touched. "You guys are in for some work."

Rick looked past her into the hallway. "Does the whole house look like this?"

"Oh, yeah. You should see the upstairs." She stepped aside to let them in. Being alone in the house all day had taken its toll. Too many unwanted memories had flooded her brain and, in truth, she was feeling a little squirrelly. She was actually grateful now for the company.

Jeff, who looked to be about fourteen years old, pulled off his ball cap. "Man, I always knew the old lady was a little creepy, but I never figured on this."

Rick jabbed his brother in the ribs. "Jeez, Jeff, shut up."

Jeff shrugged. "What? Mrs. Warren *was* creepy. She got after me just a month ago because she saw me tossing out old newspapers. Guess she had a thing for newspapers."

Rick looked at Kelsey, his eyes filled with apology. "Sorry. Most people thought a lot of Mrs. Warren."

She shrugged. "It's okay. Ruth did have a thing for paper. All kinds of paper." She glanced down the cluttered hallway. She'd ruined the neat stacks as she'd gone through the papers today. Papers were strewn everywhere. "I bought a bunch of garbage bags today."

"We can start stuffing 'em and hauling out to the truck," Rick said.

"Let's do it," Kelsey said.

The boys worked hard, hauling out garbage bags to a large beat-up pickup truck parked by the curb. By the time they'd finished, twenty bags filled the bed of the truck. Every muscle in Kelsey's body ached and the boys were covered in sweat.

"You guys have been a great help, but I know it's getting late." She found her purse hanging on the coatrack by the front door. "Let me pay you guys for your help."

Rick shook his head. "Nope, this one is on us."

Jeff grinned. "Mitch said it was a great way for us to work our way out of the doghouse."

Rick glared at his brother, his face reddening.

Kelsey couldn't help but laugh at Jeff's honesty. She met Rick's hesitant gaze. "So how'd you end up in the doghouse?"

"It was just a misunderstanding," Rick said.

"He borrowed Mom's car without asking," Jeff offered. "While he had it, he backed into another car. Cost almost a thousand dollars to fix it."

"Tough break," Kelsey said. "I took Ruth's car a time or two, though I never wrecked it." She'd taken Ruth's car out at night after her aunt had fallen asleep. She never went anywhere in particular. She just drove.

Rick looked relieved. "If Dad had been alive, Mom wouldn't have freaked so much. When she told Mitch, he had a fit."

The boys had lost their father. Her heart went out to them, but she didn't press for details. She'd always hated it when people asked her questions. "I'll bet Mitch did blow a gasket," she said, following the two boys out to the truck.

"We'll be back tomorrow," Jeff said climbing into the passenger side.

"Are you sure? You don't have to," she said. Today, she'd made three times the progress she'd expected.

Rick climbed behind the wheel. He smiled and for a moment she couldn't breathe. He was Mitch. And she was transported back to a time when she and Mitch had worked in the dive shop. He'd had that same easy grin that made her heart melt. "We'll be here." He sounded almost anxious to return.

"Heck," Jeff said, "it's kinda fun. Like a treasure hunt."

Kelsey waved as the boys drove off.

Treasure. If you could consider murder clues treasure.

# Chapter 7

By the time Mitch pulled up in front of Kelsey's house, it was past nine o'clock in the evening. The house was dark except for a light in the kitchen. He saw Kelsey's slim figure pass in front of a window. Good thing she was still up.

A dull ache had settled around his temples, and he itched to crawl into bed. He'd not had seven straight hours of sleep in two weeks.

The search for Chris had yielded nothing. The guy had simply vanished. Mitch had called Stu and informed him. The old man sounded fragile and worried, and spent several hours calling Chris's friends and family. No one had seen any sign of him. It was as if the man had fallen off the face of the earth.

Mitch strode up to the Warren house. The sound of music drifted out to greet him. Jazz. He never figured Kelsey for a jazz enthusiast. She struck him as the pop/rock type.

He knocked on the door. At first, he didn't hear footsteps and thought perhaps she hadn't heard him over the music. He knocked again.

"I heard you," she shouted over the music. "I'm coming." She turned the music down.

Kelsey opened the door. She was wearing a thick terry cloth robe and her hair was damp as if she'd just washed it. Her face was cleanly scrubbed. He held his breath for a moment, unable to find his voice.

"Kinda late, isn't it, Sheriff?" Kelsey said. Her voice was smoky, seductive and he knew he could get lost in the sound of it.

"I have news."

She nodded, the light in her eyes dying. "I didn't think that I would hear from you so soon." She stepped back and held out her arm. "Come on in."

He was struck by two things. First, the hallway was completely clean. Not only had the papers been cleaned out, but the floor had been swept. Without the clutter, the entryway was brighter, more inviting. Second was the smell of tomatoes, basil and garlic drifting from the kitchen. He remembered then that he hadn't eaten since lunch. "You've been busy."

"Your nephews were a big help. Thanks for sending them." She closed the door behind him.

Standing next to him in her bare feet, she barely reached his shoulder. Once she'd fit nicely in the crook of his arm. "They didn't give you any trouble, did they?"

"They were perfect gentlemen." She tucked a strand of hair behind her ear. A small gold hoop earring glistened from her small earlobe. "Rick told me he was on probation."

Mitch grunted. "He'll be lucky if he works off his indenture before he hits thirty."

She chuckled. "Give the kid a break. Weren't you young and stupid once?"

He didn't dare touch that one. "Look, I don't want to take up a lot of your time. I came to give you the preliminary results."

She moistened her lips. "Are you hungry?"

The question caught him off guard, but he recovered.

She wasn't ready to hear what he had to say yet. "Starving."

"Come on back to the kitchen. My marinara is almost ready and the pasta is cooked."

He followed her down the wide hallway to the kitchen. The

room was large with an overhead fluorescent light that shone down on a pink and gray Formica floor. Along the north wall was an old white stove, a wide porcelain sink with a drying rack next to it, and a narrow counter. To his right was a refrigerator that had to be fifty years old.

A gray table trimmed in dull chrome and surrounded by four matching chairs was piled high with boxes of papers, as were the far corners of the kitchen.

"Smells good." He never figured her for a cook.

There were two pots on the stove—one for sauce and one with cooked pasta glistening with butter. "I learned to cook a few dishes when I was in Italy. I got tired of eating in restaurants."

She found two bowls from the cupboard, washed them and then placed a healthy serving of pasta in each. She ladled marinara on each and grated fresh cheese and pepper on top. She handed him the bowl.

"Wine?"

"Water's good."

"Sure." She poured one glass of ice water and one red wine. "Let's go sit on the back porch and eat. Then we can talk. I haven't had a chance to clean this room yet and I get antsy around the clutter."

"Lead the way." He followed her outside and they both sat on the back step. The night was cool and the air clean. Suddenly, he could feel the tension draining from his back. He took a bite of pasta and, to his surprise, discovered it was good.

They ate in silence for several minutes, each lost in their own thoughts. Mitch liked sitting beside her. He liked having her close. The realization nearly made him laugh. What was it about him and difficult women? After he and his ex had broken up for good, he'd sworn no more complications. And here he was.

But it really wasn't fair to compare Kelsey and Alexa. Alexa was a clinger. Whether it was city life, her friends or him, she always needed someone. Kelsey had her quirks, but she could stand on her own two feet.

Kelsey set her fork down. She held the earthenware bowl in her hands, staring ahead into the dark. "The body was Donna, wasn't it?"

He set his bowl down. "Yes."

She shoved out a sigh. "It's not like I didn't know it anyway."

It was one thing to have a gut feeling. Another to have facts. "Right."

"How did she die?"

He hesitated. "We don't have the full report yet."

"But you have a theory."

He sighed. "She was shot in the chest."

She squeezed her eyes closed. "She was murdered?"

"Yes." He wanted to take her in his arms. She looked so alone and fragile at this moment. "Is there anyone I can call for you—someone you can stay with?"

She straightened her shoulders. "No, I'm good."

"Kelsey, you really shouldn't be alone."

She stood abruptly. "Thanks for everything."

He rose immediately. "Where are you going?"

She tapped her fingertips against her thigh. "I don't know. I've just got to do something."

He laid his hands on her shoulders. "You shouldn't be alone."

She glanced up at him, her eyes now watery pools. She was struggling for control. "I've been on my own most of my life. I don't need anyone, Sheriff."

He could feel the tension in her body under his fingertips. "Let me call Stu. Maybe you can spend the night with him, he could use the company. Chris is missing."

"Missing?"

"He says Chris had taken off before, but he's worried." For an instant, her gaze shifted and he thought she'd change her mind and stay with Stu.

"I'll give him a call. He's got enough on his plate. I'll get through this alone."

66

He wanted to pull her into his arms, hold her close and protect her from the pain. And for a moment, she looked up at him, her body leaning in toward him just a fraction, as if she wanted to be held.

His hands slid down to her arms with the idea of holding her, if only for a moment. She stiffened, but didn't pull away.

He leaned his head forward and touched his lips to hers. He'd forgotten how good she tasted, how much he'd enjoyed the feel of her body against his. He thought she'd let him draw her into his embrace and that the kiss would deepen. He wanted that.

But she pulled away and stepped back. She dragged her hand through her hair. "I'm tired."

She'd not allow him to comfort her no matter how much he wanted to take her misery away. His heart ached for her.

"Eventually, this is something you're going to have to work through alone. But for tonight, let me take you to Stu's."

"No."

Before he could argue, she disappeared into the house. He heard her throw the lock on the door.

As he stared at the closed back door, Mitch jabbed his fingers. He wanted to pound on the door and demand that she go to Stu's. He marched up to the door, raised his fist and then hesitated. He spread his flat palm against the door and pulled in a deep breath.

What was he doing?

She was a big girl. They'd had a past, but neither owed the other anything. So why did he feel so helpless?

"Color me one big, damn fool."

It was seven o'clock in the morning when Kelsey woke. She'd spent a long, restless night in her old bed. She tossed and turned and dreamed of Donna during a time when things had been pretty good. They'd been in California and it had been her eighth birthday. There'd been no friends to share the day with, but Donna had taken Kelsey to Disneyland. The day had been magical.

They'd laughed and Kelsey had eaten junk food until she'd had a bellyache. She'd climbed into bed that night still wearing her new Mickey Mouse T-shirt, believing that Donna had finally gotten her act together.

The next day, Donna was arrested for credit card fraud. She'd financed their outing with a card she'd stolen from some lady in Fresno. Donna made bail and they skipped town two days later.

Despite all her screwups Kelsey continued to believe that somehow, someday, Donna would get her act together.

*Donna was dead.*

Whatever doubts she'd nurtured all these years were banished by Mitch's announcement last night. Donna would never make things right between them.

She was alone.

Kelsey rubbed her temple, trying to ease the dull ache. She resisted the urge to pull the covers over her head and go back to sleep. She got out of bed, dressed and pulled back her hair. She did what she always did when she felt as if she could jump out of her skin. She worked.

Five hours later, she had tackled another room—the dining room. Most of the clutter had been newspapers and it had been easy to toss them. She'd stacked them on the front porch with a note for Rick and Jeff to haul them off.

Her stomach grumbled and she realized she still hadn't eaten. There were more rooms to be done, but she needed to take a break. She strode into the kitchen to the coffeemaker and made a strong pot. But as the machine hissed and steamed and she stared at the clutter in the room, she knew she had to get out of this house or she'd go nuts.

She couldn't breathe here.

Turning the pot off, she went upstairs, showered and dressed in a clean pair of jeans and a white T-shirt. After slipping on her clogs, she grabbed her keys and purse and headed to her car. She started the Jeep up and began driving. Before she knew it, she was parking in the scuba center's lot. Kelsey shut off the car and went inside.

The bells on the front door jingled as she entered. The shop had once been a pizza place years ago when Stu had purchased it. Now, new wet suits, flippers and masks hung where there'd been pictures of Italy; air tanks rested where the ovens had been; and a long glass display case stood where there'd been booths.

The place was quiet and there was no sign of people.

"Stu?"

He poked his head out of the back room. The instant he saw her, he grinned, went to her and hugged her. "How you doing, Kelsey?"

He was dressed in khakis and a black collared shirt with a red scuba center logo embroidered on the right breast pocket. He'd showered and combed back his gray hair. He smelled of chlorine and aftershave, as he always had. His warm embrace nearly brought her to tears.

She walked down the narrow hallway and hugged him. "I'm good."

"You sure?"

She sniffed and smiled. "Good to go." Needing to distance herself from the emotion, she pulled back and glanced around the shop. "Any word on Chris?"

His smile faded. His worry was evident. "No."

She scrambled for words of comfort. She glanced into the display case at a handful of the latest dive computers. "Any idea where Chris could be?"

He sighed. "I wish I knew. The police found his car, but there is no sign of him."

She frowned. "You know how he can just stop what he's doing and take off." He'd written about Chris's excursions often in his letters.

"The only place he went was Atlantic City. But his car was found on the *southbound* side of 81."

"He should have been on the north side."

"Exactly."

"How long has it been?"

"He left town two days ago. They found the car yesterday."

Kelsey knew how lame words of comfort could sound. And still she heard herself saying, "Hang in there. He's tough. I bet he turns up soon."

The front bells of the shop rang. Stu winked at her. "Be right back."

His gait was still stiff as he moved down the hallway to the front of the store. She'd remembered what Mitch had said about the motorist who'd nearly run him over. A chill snaked down her spine. It would have broken her heart to lose Stu.

Kelsey could hear a woman's voice up front but couldn't place it. She walked to the front of the hallway and glanced out into the store.

The woman who stood looking down at the display case was dressed for tennis, but everything about her spoke of money—her French manicured fingers, diamond bracelet, crisp white Polo shirt and pleated white tennis skirt. Her black hair was cut short, the edges spiked in a fashionable style.

Mrs. Boyd Randall. Sylvia. Kelsey had never met the woman, but knew instantly who she was. She'd seen her picture in the local paper enough times when she lived in Grant's Forge. Stu greeted Mrs. Randall.

She grinned. "Boyd's birthday is coming up and I wanted to get him something special. He's planning a dive trip to Cancun in September and I thought it would be nice if I could update some of his equipment. I spoke to Chris about this last week and he was going to order a couple of wristwatch computers for me to look at."

Stu nodded. "He did. They arrived yesterday."

"Is Chris here?" she said. "Since I started the process with him, it makes sense to finish it with him."

Stu opened the case and lined the three compact dive computers on the glass top. "Chris is in Richmond visiting his family now."

Mrs. Randall looked disappointed. "Which one of these do you recommend?"

Kelsey stayed back, pretending to study a pair of split fins hanging on the wall. Stu launched into a discussion about the pros and cons of each computer.

"Have you used any of them?" Mrs. Randall asked.

Stu shook his head. "Nope, I haven't used any of them. I have a tendency to stick with what I know."

"That's what I like about Chris. He always tries out the latest equipment." Mrs. Randall's voice was soft, but there was no missing the irritation.

Stu glanced toward Kelsey. "I bet I know someone who has used these computers. Hey, Kelsey, would you come over here for a moment?"

Damn. After her run-in with Boyd, she wasn't interested in chatting with Mrs. Randall. Kelsey let loose of the fins and walked over to the display case. She smiled at Mrs. Randall.

"Mrs. Randall, this is Kelsey Warren. She used to work in the shop and she's been diving all around the world for the last eight years. If anybody is up on the latest equipment, she is."

The woman's smile didn't falter, but for a moment, Kelsey felt a chill. The woman's gaze slid up and down Kelsey, taking in her attire and stance. She sensed she fell short in Sylvia Randall's eyes.

The moment of scrutiny passed as quickly as it came, and Sylvia recovered quickly. The perfect politician's wife, she extended her manicured hand to Kelsey.

Kelsey took Mrs. Randall's cold hand. "Hi."

"It's nice to meet you," the older woman said smoothly. "So you are the scuba expert?"

"I don't know if I'm an expert but I've dived a lot these last few years." She glanced at the three computers lying on the table. She picked up the first—a wristwatch-shaped computer. "You can't go

71

wrong with any of these, but I prefer this one. It's pricey, but it is compact. It does well at all depths and because it's lightweight, it doesn't get in the way."

Sylvia accepted the wristwatch computer and held it in her small hands. She handed it to Stu without glancing at the one-thousand-dollar price tag. "Wrap it up."

Stu grinned. "Will do."

Sylvia dug out her credit card and set it on the case. Kelsey started to ease away, feeling her duty was done.

"Thanks for the help, Kelsey," Sylvia said, as if she wasn't ready to let her slip away. "I don't know the first thing about diving, but my husband loves it."

Kelsey remembered Boyd when he'd first showed an interest in diving. He visited the dive shop while she was in school, but Stu had told her that Boyd had spent hours in the pool learning all he could about the sport. "I'm sure he'll love the computer, Mrs. Randall."

"I hope so. And please call me Sylvia."

Kelsey felt as if she should say or do something but she didn't know what. She smiled and nodded.

"You know, you look a lot like your mother," Sylvia said.

The comment caught her off guard. Not because she hadn't heard it enough, but because it seemed odd that a woman like Sylvia Randall would even know Donna. She found herself hungry for any information about her mother. "You knew my mother?"

"You sound surprised."

"It's just that you two lived pretty different lives."

Sylvia's eyes warmed. "Grant's Forge is a small town. Everyone crosses everyone's path eventually."

Their paths had never crossed until now. "Did you two go to school together?"

The questions seemed to flatter Sylvia. "Oh no, I must be a good ten or twelve years older than your mother. No, I just saw her around town."

"Oh." *And?* Kelsey waited for the other shoe to drop. Everyone had a Donna Warren story.

"I believe she worked as a waitress at the University Club when she was in high school. She was quite stunning in those days." She smiled. "Just as you are now."

"Thanks." The information explained Boyd's reaction at the diner to her crack about him knowing Donna. Rich and unavailable had been Donna's type when she was younger. As she'd aged, she'd become less choosy.

"So you've been traveling the world? How very interesting."

"I've enjoyed it." There was some kind of undercurrent, but she couldn't put her finger on it. "And where have you been?"

"Fiji, Italy, Hawaii. I hope to go to Africa this winter."

"I adore Africa. Boyd and I went on a camera safari several years ago. He wasn't so fond of the heat, but I loved the desert. Breathtaking sunsets."

"Just need your John Hancock here," Stu said, interrupting them.

Sylvia turned, signed the receipt, tore off her copy and carefully replaced both her card and folded paper in her Hermès wallet. Her movements were so precise, as if she never wasted a bit of energy.

Kelsey imagined the woman made few mistakes or did anything without thinking it through. She edged back a step, grateful not to have Sylvia's penetrating gaze studying her.

Sylvia took the package. "Well, thank you again, Stu. And Kelsey, it was a real pleasure meeting you. Are you staying in town long?"

"A few weeks, maybe a month."

Sylvia smiled again. "Well, I hope you enjoy our fair town. You certainly have chosen the best time of year to visit us."

"Thanks."

Sylvia nodded and left.

Kelsey watched Sylvia climb into her Lexus V8. Only when the woman pulled out into traffic did she turn to Stu. "That was too easy."

"What do you mean?"

"She knew Donna, and she didn't have anything bad to say."

"Not everyone hated Donna."

Her gut said otherwise. "Sylvia Randall did."

# Chapter 8

"I didn't hate Donna," Stu said softly.

Kelsey stared at Stu. He'd been the only one who hadn't. "I've been meaning to ask you why? All those years you stuck by her, sent her money or helped her out when she needed it."

Stu dropped his gaze to the register and seemed to take a sudden interest in one of the buttons. "I don't know. She just seemed like a lost soul to me."

"I never thought of her as lost so much as selfish."

He shook his head. "She wasn't always like that. When you were born, I went to see her in the hospital. She'd stand at the nursery window, just crying because she thought you were so pretty."

Kelsey had never seen her mother cry, unless she had been trying to convince a police officer to let her out of a speeding ticket. The image Stu conjured touched a part of her heart she'd long closed off. She blew out a breath to relieve the sudden pressure in her chest. She needed to change the subject. "You can bet Sylvia never saw the tender side of Donna."

He shook his head. "You're right."

Kelsey sensed Stu had left a lot unsaid and she was ready to question him further when the bells on the front door jingled. She turned and saw Mitch stride into the shop. His brown sheriff's uniform shirt stretched over his broad chest. His creases were crisp and a shiny silver badge winked in the sunlight. He pulled off his aviators and blue eyes settled on her.

Her heart kicked.

She regretted being so abrupt with him last night.

"Kelsey," Mitch said. His deep baritone voice struck a chord inside her that had her wishing she had fewer hormones and more brains.

She nodded, not quite able to trust her voice.

"Hey, Mitch," Stu said. "Got any news on Chris?"

"No."

"Stu," she said. "Is there anything I can do to help? Do you need help with the shop?"

"No way, honey," he said.

"I don't mind helping." Work kept her sane.

"You just found out your mother died, Kelsey. You just worry about yourself."

She'd had a long, good cry last night. "Donna's been out of my life for ten years. I've known all along she wasn't coming back. But this business with Chris, you just saw him a couple of days ago. You're going to find him aren't you, Mitch?"

Mitch hesitated. His expression reflected a mixture of sadness, wishful thinking and hard reality. She could see he struggled with all three. And it was that struggle that had her heart opening to him. He might have broken her heart eight years ago, but he cared about Stu. In that moment, Kelsey saw Mitch for the good, decent man he had become.

"Let's just take this a step at a time, Stu. Let me handle this," Mitch said.

Stu's shoulders slumped, as if the burden of worrying over a friend was too great for him. "Okay."

Mitch looked squarely at Kelsey. "Might not be a bad idea if you two stick together today. You're good for each other."

"Where are you headed?" she asked. It was none of her business, but a part of her wanted to delay his departure for just another moment or two.

He lifted a brow, surprised by the question. "To the quarry."

She straightened. "Why?"

"The crews from Roanoke are coming today and we're going back down to investigate."

Kelsey itched to go with him. She wanted to be a part of the investigation. She wanted to know who had shot her mother. But Stu was upset and she sensed her place was here with him.

"I don't suppose Kelsey could tag along with you?" Stu said.

Kelsey didn't hide her shock. "I thought I'd hang out with you today. I've been itching to have a look at those dive computers I saw earlier."

Stu shook his head. "I got too much work to nursemaid you." The old buzzard knew she wanted in on the investigation.

"She can't come, Stu," Mitch said.

"See, Stu?" Kelsey said, shaking off the twinge of annoyance Mitch had stirred. "The Big Bad here says I can't tag along, so I might as well stay with you."

Stu shook his head. "Now I've seen it all. Kelsey and Mitch agreeing on something."

"Don't get carried way, Stu," Kelsey said.

Stu arched a thick gray eyebrow. "You want to go?"

Yeah, sure she did. She wanted to go more than anything. "I'll stay here."

Stu looked at Mitch. "Do me a favor and get this woman out of my hair." He touched his balding head. "Or at least what's left of it. I really do have work to do. I don't want Chris returning and busting my chops for shirking."

Mitch studied the old man. The idea of taking Kelsey didn't appeal to him at all, but he wanted to help Stu out. "All right, I'll take her."

* * *

77

Neither Kelsey nor Mitch said much as he drove through the town streets toward the quarry. The day was stunning. The skies were a brilliant crystal blue, the air warm and a gentle breeze teased the tops of the trees.

Yet for all the day's beauty, Kelsey felt sick inside. Old emotions she'd tried so hard to bury bubbled to the surface, tightening her throat.

"What's wrong?" Mitch said.

His deep voice surprised her. "Nothing."

He glanced at her quickly then back to the road. "You look like you're about to jump out of your skin."

"I'm fine."

"No one's going to give you a medal for going to the quarry. Why don't you let me take you back home?"

"I'm good."

From the corner of her eye, she could see his jaw tense. "You're too damn stubborn."

She shrugged. "Not exactly breaking news."

He slowed the car and pulled off to the side of the road. "That does it."

"What!"

"When you start acting like a smart-ass, I know you're upset."

She couldn't see his eyes behind his sunglasses, but she imagined they snapped with anger. "I cracked a couple of wise remarks to ease the tension."

"You're scared."

Terrified was more like it. "I'm *fine*. But I'll admit I have a lousy sense of humor. Look, I want to go to the quarry."

"Not until you tell me what's eating you?"

If only she could. She shrugged, hoping he'd get tired of the questions and just start driving again. "*Nothing!*"

"Not good enough."

Having him this close unsettled her. "Start driving and maybe I'll start talking."

"Start talking and *maybe* I'll drive." To prove his point, he shut off the engine, leaned back in his seat and pulled off his sunglasses. "I'm all ears."

Having those blue eyes of his piercing into her didn't help at all. She sighed. "I'm just out of sorts, which I think is natural, don't you?"

"This goes beyond finding your mother's body. You were like this back . . . then."

*Then.* When they'd worked together. When they'd been lovers.

When she didn't say anything, he started to talk. "I remember a couple of the girls from high school coming into the shop around July Fourth. They acted like they were there to buy scuba equipment, but they spent most of their time talking to you."

She remembered that day very clearly. "Tammy and Mona. The evil twins."

"You were full of jokes after they left. What did they say to you?"

Her throat felt dry. "They came to invite me to a holiday lunch for mothers and daughters."

He sighed and sat back.

"Torturing me was a favorite pastime." She pushed a shaking hand through her hair. "Look, it was a long time ago and it's safe to say I took care of them both before I left town."

His eyes narrowed. "What did you do?"

Good. She'd rather talk about Tammy and Mona than Donna. "Well, if you must know, it involved lots of molasses and wood chips."

He held up his hand. "Better not tell me that one. I'm a cop."

"I'm sure the statute of limitations has expired. And it looks like Tammy's hair has grown back."

Mitch pinched the bridge of his nose. "You're doing it again."

"What?" she said in all innocence.

"Deflecting the conversation from Donna."

"Donna! God, how I wish you would just leave this alone. She's *dead*. And even if she were alive, she'd be long gone to

79

God knows where. She didn't want me. I was a thorn in her side. And if you want me to say it, I will—having a mother dump you hurts like hell."

"She didn't leave you. She was murdered."

Tears tightened her throat. "She left a hundred times before that last night. I can't tell you how many nights I sat up, scared out of my wits, waiting for her. Or how many times she didn't think to feed me. Being Donna Warren's daughter was not a happy place to be." He didn't say anything.

Just having Mitch close did something to her. For a moment, she was back in high school and in love with him. Before she thought, she said, "And God help me, but I loved my mother. I tried so hard to be good so that she'd love me like other mothers loved their children. But she never did."

His expression softened in a way that tore at her heart and made her regret her candor.

Tears filled her eyes and she looked out the passenger side window, trying her best to tamp down the emotions. "I should punch you, Mitch Garrett."

"Why?" he said softly.

"Because I don't cry and I sure don't wallow in sloppy emotions."

"Maybe you should."

"I've never talked to anyone about this stuff."

"Again, maybe you should." He laid his hand on her shoulder. Warmth and strength from his fingertips seeped into her shoulder.

A tear fell down her cheek and she viciously swiped it away. "Talk doesn't mean anything to me. I got a bellyful of *talk* from Donna over the years. Action is what I respect."

Gently, he placed his hand on her chin and turned her face toward him. She didn't resist. He leaned closer to her, resting his hand on the back of the seat. "I will find your mother's killer."

The steel behind his words almost had her believing him. "Don't make promises you can't keep, Sheriff."

He didn't flinch. "I never do."

"It's been ten years. She's been at the bottom of the quarry all that time. A case doesn't get any colder." He possessed a strength about him that made him think he could conquer anything. But she wasn't a teenager in need of rescue anymore.

"If you haven't noticed, I'm stubborn," he said softly. "And I gravitate toward the tough cases."

"Like me."

"Yep."

His hand shifted a fraction and lightly touched the tips of her hair. If she'd not been so focused on him, she might have missed it. It would have been easy to ignore. All she'd have had to do was shift her position slightly and the connection would have been broken. Mitch wouldn't have pushed it. It would all have been forgotten.

But Kelsey didn't move away.

She moved a fraction closer to him so that his knuckle brushed the side of her ear.

Mitch stared at her. He didn't move.

All he had to do now was lean over and kiss her. And she'd let him. Losing herself in sex appealed to her more than she could say.

Anticipation had her heart thundering, left her mouth dry. So easy. So easy.

"No." She couldn't believe what she just said.

He eased back a fraction. "Okay."

The survival instinct buried deep inside her had taken over, understanding that she couldn't let herself fall for Mitch again. When they parted, and they would, it would shatter her. "I think we better get to the quarry."

He didn't seem offended as he started the engine. "You're right." He checked for traffic and then pulled out onto the road. "Because when I do kiss you, there'll be nothing standing between us."

*　*　*

Mitch drove into the quarry entrance and was still very aware of Kelsey. He didn't know what had happened back there with her, but whatever it was had kicked him in the gut.

He drove down to the parking area and shut off the car. The recovery crews had already gathered around the edge of the quarry. They were dressed in dry suits, designed to keep divers warm at greater depths.

Kelsey noticed the suits as well. "Dry suits? That means they're diving into the crevice."

"Yep." He put the car in Park and shut off the engine.

"Do you really think they'll find anything?"

"I'll let you know."

A slight frown creased her forehead. "You're going, too?"

He didn't want to leave her. "Not unless I hurry." He imagined he saw a flash of worry in her eyes. Did she want to say something else to him?

After a pause, she said, "Then I guess you better get going."

"Right." He was tempted to bag the dive, because he sensed Kelsey needed him. Of course, hell would freeze over before she asked, but he knew her emotions were a raw nerve now.

She opened her door and walked to the back of the Suburban, as if needing fresh air and space. "Let me help you with your gear."

Kelsey was pushing him away. She was good at that.

Mitch met her at the tailgate. He opened the door and yanked out his gear.

As much as he wanted to give in to his urge to stay behind, she was right to give him the shove. He wanted in on this dive. He wanted to see the bottom of the crevice with his own eyes to make sure nothing was missed. He owed that much to Kelsey. "I'll be back as soon as I can."

She smiled and nodded her head as if she didn't care one way or the other if she ever saw him again. "I'll be here."

\* \* \*

Kelsey stood on the edge of the quarry.

Mitch and the other divers had been underwater for fifteen minutes. They'd be up very soon. The divers were in the crevice, which had to be over one hundred feet deep. Using Nitrox, a mixture of oxygen and nitrogen, in their tanks, they could stay at the deeper depth longer than the average recreational diver. But even with the Nitrox, they couldn't stay down longer than twenty more minutes.

The police pontoon boat was moored in the center of the lake and an officer sat in the boat, waiting for the divers. It was almost a replay of Sunday.

Kelsey hugged her arms around her chest. A gentle breeze wafted along the trees rimming the quarry's north face, which rose a hundred feet higher than the south end where she stood. The leaves rustled. The breeze should have felt good in the hot sun, but her skin was chilled. Cold quarry waters lapped at her feet.

Her skin prickled and her heart began to race. It felt as if someone were watching her. She glanced toward the policeman, but he was staring into the water, waiting for signs of his divers.

For unknown reasons, her gaze was drawn to the center of the north rim above the quarry. Thick dense trees ringed the land above the granite walls. She couldn't see past the dense vegetation, but she kept staring.

She imagined she saw the shrubs move as if someone were walking along the ridge. She couldn't tear her gaze from the crest. An unsettling fear had her taking a couple of steps back.

"You're being silly, Kelsey," she whispered. She started to turn when a flash of light from the ridge caught her eye. She froze. *Someone was up there!*

Irritated by her fear, she moved back to the edge of the water, searching harder for another flash or a rustle of movement that would prove someone was moving around up there.

"Hey!" she called out to the policeman. "Did you see a flash on the ridge?"

He shook his head no and turned back toward the water.

"Of course you didn't see it. I'm turning into a paranoid freak that gets spooked by the wind," she muttered.

She shoved her hands in her pockets. "Hurry up, Mitch."

Mitch and the men came up twenty minutes later. Mitch took off his equipment. Instantly, she could see he wasn't happy. Grim-faced, he strode toward her.

Water dripped from his suit and the chill from the greater depths still clung to him. "Let's head back to the car," Mitch said when he reached her.

"Why?" He was trying to get rid of her—which was all the more reason to dig in her heels, even if this place gave her the spooks.

He yanked off his hood. "For once, would you just do as I say?"

She shot him a you've-got-to-be-kidding glare before her gaze skipped from him across the water to the police boat.

There were three divers in the boat. They had taken off their tanks and unzipped the tops of their suits. All three men were pulling on a rope.

Suddenly, a figure wrapped in ropes and an algae-covered tarp floated to the surface. The officers secured it to the side of the pontoon and started toward shore.

The color drained from her face. There was no mistaking what it was.

They'd found another body.

# Chapter 9

"Do you have any idea who it is?" Kelsey asked.

"No. By the looks of it, the body hasn't been in the water as long . . ." Mitch let his words trail off.

"As my mother," she said finishing his sentence. "Lose the kid gloves, Mitch. I'll deal with all this a lot better if you don't treat me like a wimp."

"Right." No anger, just understanding in his gaze as he shifted it to the water. "If I had to guess, I'd say this body has been in the water at least three years."

"How long before you can identify the body?"

"Unless there is some clue on the body that helps us along, it could be weeks, maybe never."

"You identified Donna so quickly."

"Based on your hunch, the medical examiner checked your mother's dental records first. He was as surprised as anyone that he had a hit on the first try." He rubbed the back of his neck with his hand. "Do me a favor and keep all this quiet. I don't need a thousand tourists down here trying to dive these waters. Two bodies are too much of a coincidence."

"Are you saying whoever killed Donna killed this person?"

"I don't know. We'll wait until the autopsy."

She glanced over his shoulder at the tarp-wrapped body lying on the beach. An odd sensation tickled the back of her neck. "At least it's not Chris."

Her relief lasted until she looked up toward the ridge. Uneasiness settled in her bones. "I saw a flash of light on the ridge while you were in the water. Did you have a policeman up there?" She wasn't sure why she mentioned it to Mitch. Maybe she wanted him to tell her not to worry so she could convince herself that her imagination had just gotten the better of her.

Frowning, his gaze shifted to the ridge. "There were no policemen up there."

"I thought I saw someone up on the ridge watching me. Must have been my imagination."

Mitch continued to stare up at the ridge, guiding Kelsey toward his car. "Give me a second." He reached for his radio. "Mabel?"

After a pause, "Yeah, boss."

"Do we have anyone available to ride up to the north ridge of the quarry and have a look around?"

Kelsey felt color rise in her cheeks. "Mitch," she whispered, "this really isn't necessary. It was probably my imagination."

He winked at her. "Doesn't hurt to look."

The radio crackled with Mabel's voice, "George is free and is now on his way."

"Great. Have him call me when he's done a walkover."

"Will do."

Mitch replaced the radio. "Let me change and we can head back to town."

She glanced up toward the north ridge. No lights flashed. No leaves rustled. "I felt like a fool for even saying anything."

"Don't sweat it."

Few people had ever taken Kelsey seriously when she'd lived in Grant's Forge. But Mitch had. Even in the old days, he'd listened to her rattle on about her dreams and he had encouraged her to reach for them.

It was just one more reason why she'd fallen in love with him. And why she could again if she wasn't careful.

She walked away from the Suburban while he changed. He needed privacy, and she needed distance. She jabbed her fingers through her hair.

The guy takes her seriously and she goes all weak in the knees. She reminded herself that other men who'd known her professionally had also taken her seriously—*because* she was smart and only spoke when she had something to say.

She glanced over at Mitch as he toweled off his face.

*Love.*

This could not be happening again. *It would not happen.*

Kelsey didn't see or hear from Mitch over the next three days. She was glad for the break. The distance gave her a chance to steady her shaky emotions and to get her balance back.

Donna's body had still not been released for burial, so she spent the time cleaning Ruth's house. She spoke to her magazine editor once and, against her better judgment, turned down an assignment in Bali.

Each day, the boys showed up after school, cleaned with her for a few hours and then hauled away the mountains of paper Ruth had collected over the years. Kelsey had worked hard on the house and by week's end, the downstairs had been stripped of the clutter.

So far, she'd found nothing to tell her anything about Donna. She tossed stacks of newspapers, the box of utility bills that dated back to the 1950s, and more phone books than she'd ever seen, even in the New York Public Library.

The work was good for her. She felt a sense of accomplishment and triumph with each garbage bag she dragged out of the house.

On the fourth day, she was even feeling like she'd kicked this mini obsession she had for Mitch Garrett. She only thought about him two or three times a day, instead of six or seven as she had on the first day. And she was only a little put out by the fact that he hadn't called.

When her cell phone rang unexpectedly, she was in the den. The cell was in the kitchen. She vaulted over two boxes, sprinted down the hallway and banged her knee on the kitchen table as she answered the phone on the fifth ring.

"Hello," she said breathless.

"Kelsey," Stu said.

She allowed a tiny bit of disappointment before she shrugged it off. Okay, no Mitch. What did she care? "Stu, how are you?"

"Chris still hasn't turned up." Worry coated each word.

"What's it been, five days?" she asked.

"Yeah."

"No word from the police?"

"They haven't found a trace of him. I've checked all the hospitals in the state and no one has seen him."

"That's a good sign, right?"

"I suppose."

She reached for a cup of coffee left over from breakfast. "Chris is known to take off, Stu."

"Not like this."

She took a sip. The coffee was cold. "Hey, why don't we meet for dinner? We could go into town and I'll treat you to dinner at that Italian place you used to like. It's still there, isn't it?"

"Yeah, it's still there, but we'll never get close to town tonight."

She set the coffee down. "Why?"

"It's Memorial Weekend, Kelsey." He sounded as if he was talking to a small child.

"Oh, I'd forgotten all about that."

"They block the streets off. Bands play and the police department sets off fireworks."

"The police department" was code for Mitch Garrett, no doubt. It was on the tip of her tongue to ask Stu if Mitch was going to be there, but she held off. What did it matter who set off the fireworks?

"Yeah, I went to one of those parties years ago." Ruth had known everyone in town and had always had a blast, but Kelsey had never felt right there. She didn't belong around real families. "Well, maybe you could come by here and I could cook you supper. I make a mean Thai dish."

He hesitated. "We should go to the festival."

She stepped out the back door, needing fresh air. She leaned against the round wood column and stared up at the brilliantly blue sky. "I don't know, Stu. I'm not one for crowds."

"It would do us both good to get out and stop moping about our problems."

The edge of sadness in his voice was what got her. She couldn't say no when he was so worried and feeling so lost. "Could we go early?" And miss the crowds.

"How about six?" His voice sounded a little lighter.

She dug her fingernail under a chipping piece of paint on the column and flicked it off. Damn. "Six it is," she said brightly. "How about I meet you at the Town Square Café?"

Stu laughed. "It's not an execution, Kelsey. It'll be fun."

"Right."

"See you at the square."

She hung up to the sound of Stu chuckling. She picked another piece of paint, and then another off the column before she caught herself. At the rate she was going she'd have the back porch stripped by dinner.

Six o'clock. That gave her three hours. Three hours to shift through more papers, shower and worry if she was going to run into Mitch.

Kelsey spent more time choosing an outfit than she had buying her first camera. In the end, she chose to go simple—jeans, a white cotton shirt and black slides. She skipped her bracelets and pulled her hair back, thinking it made her look more conservative. And then she caught herself. Why was she trying to fit in with these people? She brushed out her hair. Rebellion simmering in her veins, she put on her bracelets and added a couple of extras for good measure. She considered a mock nose ring but decided that was too over the top. Besides, the darn thing pinched.

Traffic would be a crush, so she opted to walk the nine blocks into town. She grabbed her digital camera and put fresh batteries in it. It made no sense to photograph anything today, but habits were a hard thing to break. Her camera was her safety blanket.

She locked her front door. As she moved across the front porch, she spotted a lovely white bag with a pink ribbon wrapped around it. At first, she thought Jeff or Rick had left her something. Jeff had confessed yesterday that Rick had a crush on her. Curious and oddly touched, she picked it up. She untied the ribbon and draped it carefully over the porch rail.

Inside the bag was an old Kewpie doll, not bigger than the size of her palm. The doll's blond wavy hair had been chopped off and its eyes had been blacked out with a magic marker. She flipped the doll over. Scribbled on the doll's back were the words *Go Away*.

A chill snaked up her spine.

This was no gift.

Kelsey looked in the bag to see if her "admirer" had left a note. There was none.

The hairs on the back of her neck rose, just as they had at the quarry when she'd seen the flash of light. She glanced up and looked around, half expecting someone to be standing close by staring at her. No one was there.

"If you think I'm spooked," she said in a clear voice, "I'm not."

Kelsey shoved the doll into the bag along with the ribbon and walked around the side of the house to the trash can. She tossed it all away. "The last thing I need is a smart-ass prankster."

Rubbing trembling hands over her hips, she backed away from the trash can. Her heart hammered against her ribs and the bit of excitement she'd had moments ago for the picnic had vanished. If not for Stu, she'd have skipped the festival and gone to a movie.

She arrived at the square pavilion at five minutes after six. The nine-block walk had gone a long way to calming her nerves, but she was still rattled.

Stu stood out front, wearing his blue Hawaiian shirt, white Bermudas and flip-flops.

"Aloha," she said, approaching with the brightest smile she could conjure up.

Stu grinned. "Aloha to you." He glanced down at the tangle of bracelets on her arm. "You could pick up radio signals with those things."

She lifted her bracelet up to her mouth. "Beam me up, Scotty."

His belly laugh reminded her of the old Stu. "Nope, you're not getting out of this picnic. I plan to show you off."

"Me?"

"Sure. You're my little girl." He blushed. "At least, I've always thought about you that way."

Her throat tightened with unexpected tears and for a moment she couldn't speak, much less come up with a smart remark to bail her out. "I wish you had been my father."

His eyes softened. He hugged her. "Me, too."

She cleared her throat. "Okay, stop. I don't want to cry."

Stu grinned. "Hey look, there's Mitch."

She glanced up a little too quickly and saw him over by the Dixieland band. He was wearing his uniform and talking to Tammy Fox.

Crap. Out of the frying pan, into the fire.

Mitch glanced up and for a moment his gaze locked onto hers. A restlessness stirred inside, as if she were standing on the edge of a cliff. *Danger, Will Robinson! Danger!*

But like a deer caught in headlights, she could do nothing but stare back.

Tammy said something that jerked his attention away. Reluctantly, he looked away from her.

Kelsey turned away. She felt breathless, as if she'd run six miles. "Stu, let's head across to the other side of the park where the exhibits are."

Stu looked over at Mitch and then at her. "You mean away from Mitch."

"Don't push me, old man. I'm small, but I could take you," she grumbled.

He laughed. "Not on your best day."

The two wound their way through the park, toward the exhibits. The last time Kelsey had been to the fair, the exhibits had been on card tables set up by local farmers who displayed homemade jams, breads and crafts. Now, neat rows of large white tents with laser-printed signs were filled with trendy artisans and their work.

She pulled out her camera and started to snap pictures. There was something very quaint and fairy-tale-like about this festival. She could think of several style magazines that might be interested in the pictures. Underwater shots were her specialty, but it never hurt to try new things.

"Grant's Forge is coming up in the world," Kelsey said as she stopped in front of a potter's booth.

"We have a professional crew from D.C. come in and set it all up."

"When did this all change?"

"Seven or eight years ago, when Sylvia Randall became the chairman of the fair committee. She said folks in Washington like the country charm of our products but what they really wanted was to buy art. She opened up the fair to artisans in the region. We're a genuine art show now. Sylvia got us written up in the *Washington Post* last year—big spread in the Style section."

Kelsey moved to a booth filled with Quaker-style baskets. "Looks like it's a hit."

"Our revenue tripled since we changed our format."

"The jams and jellies had their charm. Mrs. Heckman gave me a jar of her peppermint jelly." The jelly had tasted awful, but Kelsey had been so touched by the woman's generosity, she'd kept the jar in Ruth's refrigerator until it turned moldy.

"The local vendors are here, too, but they're not assigned the prime spots. Sylvia Randall isn't always nice, but she is one shrewd businesswoman." He nodded to a spot behind Kelsey. "There she is now."

She looked down the row of booths and spotted Sylvia and Boyd. Clipboard in hand, Sylvia was dressed in a yellow cotton sundress. Manicured pink toenails peaked out of white open sandals. She'd pulled her blond hair back in a neat ponytail. Boyd, dressed in his usual khakis, white collared shirt and loafers, talked to a vendor and grinned like a Cheshire cat.

"They look so perfect. Like they came off the top of a cake." Kelsey snapped a picture of them talking to a painter.

"Image is everything."

"I suppose."

"Stu!" a vendor who sold planters shouted.

Stu turned and raised his hand. "Hey, Phil. Kelsey, I'll be right back. I want to visit with Phil."

"Oh, sure, go ahead." Leave me with the sharks. "I'll be fine."

Stu limped off toward Phil's while Kelsey started to meander down the rows of exhibits. The smell of cotton candy and the sound of the Dixieland band drifted around her.

Before she realized it, she stood in front of the Reelect Sheriff Mitch Garrett booth manned by Tammy and Bill Fox.

Bill had taken Kelsey out on a date at the beginning of senior year in high school. When she'd refused to sleep with him, he'd told everyone in school she was a tramp. What had already been a miserable high school experience turned torturous.

Walking faster, Kelsey kept her gaze ahead, hoping they wouldn't notice her.

93

"Kelsey!" Tammy cooed. "Good to see you again."

Tammy wore a pink maternity top with a ruffled collar. Bill, who'd been on the football team, had traded his muscled abs for a paunch. His once electric-blue eyes had dulled.

"Hey," Kelsey said, hoping that would be the end of their conversation.

Bill straightened his shoulders and sucked in his stomach a fraction. "Kelsey Warren, is that you?"

She stopped, not sure why she even bothered. "One and the same."

Tammy handed Kelsey a flyer. "I guess you won't be around in November when we have the election, but what the heck."

Kelsey glanced down at the pamphlet in her hand. Reelect Garrett hovered over a headshot of Mitch that stared back up at her. "Thanks."

"Good picture of him, don't you think?" Bill said. "I took it."

"Really?" It was a "grip and grin" shot and Mitch looked as if he'd been backed up against a wall and was about to be shot.

"I'm not a professional like you, but I like to dabble. Folks say my stuff is good."

"Oh, great."

Bill's gaze traveled up and down her body. "I gotta say, you look great, Kelsey."

Tammy glanced at her husband. Her eyes narrowed, and she wrapped her arm possessively around her husband. "Hey, Kelsey, take a picture of us."

"Oh sorry, my battery just died," she lied.

"Too bad," Billy said. "So what kind of camera is that?"

Before she could answer, Tammy said, "So, Kelsey, how long are you staying in town?"

"I don't know. A few weeks, maybe."

"That's all?" Tammy said. "I'd think you'd at least stick around for your mother's funeral."

Kelsey didn't reply, pretending she hadn't heard and hoping Tammy would get the hint and back off.

Tammy didn't get the hint. "So what brings you to the fair? Kind of a family type of affair."

Ah, there was the old Tammy Kelsey knew and loved. "Just killing time."

Kelsey half expected Tammy to toss a mutilated Kewpie doll at her. The sneaky stuff had been her style back in high school.

"We bad pennies show up where you least expect it. Like Kewpie dolls."

Tammy's sharp gaze clouded with confusion. She recovered her fangs. "Yeah, but why bother with a *family* event like this?"

Kelsey shrugged, her easy grin warring with the knot in her stomach. Before she could speak, Mitch strode up.

Mitch stood next to Kelsey, his shoulder brushing hers. "Kelsey is joining my family tonight, Tammy."

Tammy's satisfied grin melted. "Oh."

Kelsey glanced at Mitch. Where the devil had he come from? Seeing Tammy taken down a peg was worth having Mitch come to her rescue. "It's been ages since I've seen the Garretts. I'm looking forward to catching up," Kelsey said.

Tammy's eyes hardened. "It sounds lovely."

Bill winked at Kelsey. "Any time you want to stop by the booth and help hand out flyers, feel free."

This night was getting better and better. "Sure."

Irritated she'd gotten herself into this small-town drama, Kelsey started to walk away. Mitch fell in step behind her.

"You look like you could eat nails," he said. Laughter laced his words.

"I could."

"You're heading in the wrong direction."

She didn't even glance up at him. "This is the way back to Ruth's."

"My family is over there."

"Well, then you best run along and join them."

"I thought you were joining us."

95

She stopped in front of a Soft Serve Ice Cream truck and looked up at him. "I appreciate you bailing me out there with the Queen of the Damned and her husband, but I don't do the family thing."

He leaned toward her a fraction. "Then why come at all?"

"I don't know. Stu needed cheering up." She spotted Stu by the Dixieland band. He was clapping and singing along with a friend. "But he looks like he's having a good time and doesn't need me anymore."

"Good, then you can spend time with my bunch." He cupped his hand over her elbow and leaned closer so that his lips were close to her ear. "Besides, it'll drive Tammy nuts."

A firm no was on the tip of Kelsey's tongue when she glanced up and saw Tammy with a handful of leaflets headed their way. "Sold," Kelsey said.

# Chapter 10

Norman Rockwell couldn't have painted a better family picture.

The Garrett clan was gathered under an old oak tree on a collection of blankets and patchwork quilts. There had to be a dozen children, from ages one to sixteen, running around. The littlest one, a towheaded boy, had his mother shadowing him as he toddled about. When he stumbled she scooped him up and kissed him on the cheek. Giggling, the child arched his back, anxious to be set down again.

Kelsey's heart tightened.

Mitch's hand touched her lightly on the elbow, drawing her gaze up to his. "That's my sister Caitlin, and the Tasmanian Devil she's chasing is Robbie. He just turned a year old."

Caitlin shared Mitch's dark hair and her blue eyes sparked with curiosity as she glanced between the two of them. "Hey, guys."

Mitch winked at Robbie. "Caitlin, this is Kelsey."

"Good to meet you," Caitlin said, as if she genuinely meant it. "Mitch says you'll be joining us for dinner."

When had he said that? "Oh, right. Thanks for having me."

"The more, the merrier," Caitlin said. Robbie arched again. "I better let this fellow burn some steam. Hopefully, he'll run out of gas soon. Then I can rejoin the adult population and have a civilized conversation."

Kelsey laughed.

The news of Kelsey's arrival washed over the group like a wave. She and Mitch had barely taken steps when they were surrounded by all the Garretts. She met Mitch's oldest sister, Brenda, mother to Jeff and Rick; his two younger brothers, Quinn and Redmond, both home on leave from the Navy; and his youngest sister, Anne.

When all the siblings, nieces and nephews had been introduced, Mitch's parents moved from their post at the grill.

Mr. Garrett was as tall as Mitch and his shoulders just as broad. His black hair had thinned but he remained trim. He wore an apron that said Reelect Garrett. Mrs. Garrett was almost as tall as her husband. She was dressed in crisp white shorts and a blue denim shirt. Her salt-and-pepper hair complimented her blue eyes and olive skin.

"So who do we have here?" Mrs. Garrett said.

"Dad and Mom, this is Kelsey Warren."

Mrs. Garrett smiled warmly. "I was sorry to hear about your aunt and your mother."

For the first time, Kelsey felt as if the condolences were heartfelt. "Thanks, Mrs. Garrett."

"Oh, dear Lord, call me Sue. My mother-in-law is *Mrs.* Garrett." Kelsey laughed.

Mr. Garrett held out his large hand and when she accepted it, he wrapped warm strong fingers around her hand. "Good to have you aboard, Kelsey. I'm Ken. As you can see, things get a little zooey around here so just dive in and make yourself at home."

Sue glanced at Kelsey's camera. "I hear you are a photographer."

"Yes, underwater shots mostly. But I always carry my camera with me."

"How do you like your burger?" Ken said. "Medium," Kelsey said.

"Medium it is," Ken said flipping a burger onto the grill.

"Help yourself to sodas," Sue said. "There's a cooler by the picnic table."

Kelsey felt as if she'd been pulled into a current. "Please don't trouble yourselves."

Sue and Ken waved away her protests and returned to the grill.

"This is very kind of your parents to include me," Kelsey said.

"They like you," Mitch replied easily.

Kelsey didn't have time to react to that bit of news. A girl of about ten years old ran up to them. She had short dark hair and wore black soccer shorts and a T-shirt that said Designed For Soccer. "Hey, would you take my picture?"

Mitch raised an eyebrow. "This is my niece Morgan. Say hello before you start asking for favors, kid."

Morgan scrunched up her face at Mitch but when she faced Kelsey, she was all smiles. "Hello," the child said. "Could you take my picture, please?"

Kelsey smiled. "Sure." The girl smiled a wide gap-toothed grin and Kelsey snapped a couple of pictures. "Want to see what you look like?"

"Sure!"

Kelsey knelt down and flipped the switch on the back from Photo to View. A picture of the girl appeared. The child's eyes were closed. Kelsey scrolled through the five she'd taken, settling on the fourth which was the best.

"Hey, that's cool," Morgan said excitedly.

"When I can get to a photo shop, I'll make you a copy." Kelsey turned the camera off and stood.

The girl looked at her as if she'd just promised her the moon. "Thanks!"

"Don't worry about the photo," Mitch said. "She'll have forgotten about it tomorrow."

Kelsey tucked her camera back in its case. "I said I'd get the photo and I will."

He stared at her as if he were trying to see inside her brain. She sensed a tenderness there that made her very uncomfortable.

"So are you here in an official capacity?" she asked. She hated silence and always did her best to fill it.

"It's every man or woman on deck during this event. It's crowded tonight, but tomorrow will be a crush when the day-trippers come in from D.C. for the art show."

He reached in the cooler and pulled out two sodas. "Diet or regular?"

"Regular."

He handed her the can and kept the diet for himself. "Our biggest problems are traffic, drunks and the occasional fight."

Kelsey popped the tab and took a sip. "Sounds pretty routine."

"After this last week, routine suits me just fine."

"Any word on the other body?"

"The medical examiner says female, mid-thirties at death and in the water about five years. But there's nothing else. The body had been stripped clean of all clothing and identification."

She circled the rim of the soda can with her fingertip. "Someone didn't want her identified."

"No. They sure didn't."

Two five-year-old boys ran past them, shooting water guns at each other. The children squealed with reckless excitement.

Mitch shook his head. "Today isn't about murders. And I promised myself I'd keep it light when I saw you."

She thought about mentioning the Kewpie doll with the blackened eyes sitting on her porch. A chill slithered through her veins. She decided to keep it to herself. Mitch had enough on his plate; he didn't need to worry about some sick prank that most likely meant nothing. "Sounds like a solid plan."

"So are you up for a burger? I've got to eat ahead of the crew so I can get back to work."

"Sounds good." Excitement she'd not felt in years thrummed through her veins. Her first urge was to tamp it down, but then she decided to savor it. Tomorrow, the fairy tale would end, but for tonight she would go with the flow.

They got their burgers from Ken and sat at the picnic table. Kelsey bit into the burger and discovered it was delicious.

"So where's your next assignment?" Mitch said.

"As a matter of fact, I had an offer to go to Bali yesterday."

"And?" She couldn't read his reaction.

"I turned it down. There are just too many unresolved questions here that I want to see through."

He picked up a potato chip off his plate. "I was in the South Pacific when I was in the Navy. It's beautiful there."

She nodded. Silence settled between them. "Looks like you've got a lot of campaign volunteers."

"Family, mostly."

"And Tammy."

"She loves to organize and is good at it. She wanted to run the campaign and I don't have time for it. Seemed a natural fit."

Tammy had always had an angle. "I'm sure she'll do a great job for you."

More silence. Seemed every subject between them had a land mine attached to it. Morgan ran up to the table, her lips now purple from a grape soda. Kelsey had never been so glad to see anyone in her life.

"Uncle Mitch?"

"What is it, peanut?"

"I heard Grandma and Grandpa talking."

He settled his gaze on the child. "You're not supposed to listen in on folks."

Kelsey sipped her soda. The kid itched to share what she'd heard.

Morgan grinned and sat next to Mitch. "I know."

Mitch sighed, realizing the kid wasn't going anywhere. "Out with it."

"Grandma wants to know if you are going to marry Kelsey."

101

Kelsey started to choke on her soda.

Mitch calmly patted her on the back until she stopped. "All right, Kelsey?"

Her eyes watered, but she could breathe. She nodded.

Mitch glared down at Morgan, who didn't seem the least bit concerned. "Shove off, kid, before I lock you in jail."

Her eyes brightened. "Hey, would you? I haven't been to the jail in a long time."

"Go!" he ordered.

Giggling, she ran back toward a group of her cousins, clearly to report back.

"Good kid," Mitch said. "And a real brat at times."

"She's okay." She shook her head and laughed.

"What's so funny?"

"Marriage. The word had never been associated with my name."

He bit into his burger.

Nervous, she kept talking when she knew in her heart she should just shut up. "The most permanent thing in my life is my cell phone number and email address. My friends say I'll never get married."

Calmly, he set his burger down and wiped his hands with a napkin. "Like the old saying goes: Never say never." He tossed his napkin down. "I've got to get out a patrol for the next couple of hours. Why don't you come with me?"

"Me?"

His eyes danced with laughter. "It's either patrol or stay here and get grilled about your intentions toward me."

"Patrol sounds good."

Mitch grinned. "Smart woman." He raised his hand and waved to his father. "We'll be back in about a half-hour."

His father raised his spatula. "Ice cream will be ready in an hour."

"Will do."

Kelsey fell in step beside Mitch. His back was military straight, but he walked with an easy confidence that she couldn't help but like.

He waved to several people who smiled. Those same smiles vanished when gazes shifted to Kelsey.

"I'm not winning you any popularity contests," she said as they reached the end of the art exhibits.

He placed his hand gently on her elbow as he moved her out of the way of two pre-teens hurrying toward the center gazebo. "I can handle it."

The warmth of his fingers spread up her arm and when he released her she felt a twinge of disappointment. "A few have asked me how long I'm going to stay. They can't wait for me to leave."

"You worry too much."

She caught sight of a woman who was staring at her and shaking her head. When Kelsey's gaze locked on the woman's, the woman held it for a moment, then looked away. "I doubt it."

"Find anything interesting in your aunt's house?"

She thought about the Kewpie doll on the front porch. "Tons of paper."

"Nothing about your mother?"

"Not yet. I've decided to tackle the attic tomorrow. Should be a treat."

"If it's like my folks' attic, it will be daunting."

"I peeked up there late today. It's worse."

"Let me know if you need help."

The idea tempted her. "Thanks, I've got it under control."

Mitch spotted an older man dressed in khakis and a golf shirt, swaying as he walked toward his car. "Looks like Sam had too much at the nineteenth hole before he came to the picnic."

Kelsey held back while Mitch strolled over to the man. Mitch talked quietly to Sam as he fumbled with his keys. She couldn't hear what Mitch was saying, but there was a set to his jaw that suggested he wouldn't compromise. Sam finally handed Mitch his keys and Mitch radioed for a police car. When the car arrived, Sam got into the back and Mitch returned to Kelsey's side.

"Off to the pokey," she said jokingly.

"Nope. He's on his way home."

"So do you have a sign somewhere that says Chief Cook and Bottle Washer?"

He laughed as they continued to walk along the perimeter of the park. His deep laugh reverberated through her body. It also transformed him. It softened the hardness of his jaw and eased the furrows in his brow. He was more attractive to her now than he had ever been. Music and laughter drifted around them. "I should."

She cleared her throat. "Looks like Grant's Forge is lucky to have you."

He raised an eyebrow. "Is that a compliment?"

She shrugged. "Maybe."

The laughter in Mitch's eyes vanished as he stared down at her. The look that replaced it was more serious and it touched something deep inside her she'd thought long dead. She leaned toward him slightly. She wanted to know what it would feel like to kiss him. Would it be as good as it had been years ago? His body tensed and he took her hand in his. His fingers were warm and calloused. She could feel the strength radiating from them.

"Hey, Uncle Mitch," Morgan, his niece shouted.

Kelsey straightened, as if she'd been caught with her hand in the cookie jar.

Mitch hesitated before he released her hand. He turned toward the girl. "What's up, brat?"

"Grandpa says the homemade ice cream is done and if you don't come now, he'll feed it to the dogs."

Mitch laughed. "Kelsey, you willing to risk some family meddling for ice cream?"

"Sounds dangerous. But I think I can handle it."

The tension between them melted. And she couldn't have been more relieved. She'd set her foot on an old, dangerous path that she knew led to nowhere.

Stu intercepted them and visited for a few minutes before he made his excuses and slipped away. Kelsey insisted on walking him home, but he flatly refused.

Mitch didn't give her time to overanalyze. He walked her back to the Garrett family and spent the next several hours with them. To Kelsey's surprise, she had a good time. Mitch had to leave several times to make his patrol, and she felt comfortable staying with his family.

His brothers entertained her with stories of his childhood, his mother asked genuine questions about her and about her work, and the children continued to mug for photos. By the time Mitch returned just after the fireworks display, her camera battery was dead and her face ached from so much smiling.

She and Mitch helped Mrs. Garrett clean up and repack the massive coolers with the now-empty Tupperware dishes. He loaded the coolers into his mother's station wagon.

Kelsey hugged her arms around her chest as Mitch strode toward her. She didn't want the evening to end, but she'd learned long ago not to regret endings. They were a part of life.

"Thanks for a great evening," she said.

"Pleasure was mine."

The music had stopped, the art vendors had packed up their work and most of the families had left. "Well, I better take off. I got a full day's work ahead of me tomorrow."

"Let me drive you," he said.

She shook her head. "Thanks, but the walk will do me good."

He pulled his keys from his pocket. "It's just a ride, not a marriage proposal."

Nervous laughter bubbled from her. "Okay, fine."

Mitch walked her to his car and unlocked it with his keyless entry. Before he could reach the car, she opened her door and climbed in the front seat. Shaking his head, he walked to his side, climbed in and started the engine.

The drive to her house took less than five minutes. He parked the car, shut off the engine and climbed out as if knowing she'd tell him not to walk her to her door.

He reached her as she climbed out. He shut the door for her and together they walked to the front porch. She fumbled for her keys and unlocked the door.

She faced him. The single porch light glowed above, making the hard planes of his face look sharper. Her mouth felt dry. "I had a good time."

"Me, too."

He maintained a few inches distance between them and she knew this was her out. She could escape into the house now. But his scent circled her, drawing her closer. A sensible woman would leave while the getting was good. "You've a nice family," she said, wishing she was a wittier person.

He cupped his hand on her elbow. He'd given her the chance to leave and she'd not taken it. "They like you."

The warmth of his body beckoned her. "You're lucky to have them."

Gently, he tugged her the last inch. Her chest touched his. She gazed up into his eyes, her heart hammering in her chest.

He placed his other hand on her shoulder and leaned down and gently pressed his lips to hers. He tasted salty, sweet, dangerous. Good sense abandoned her. And she wrapped her arms around his neck and pressed her body closer to him.

Mitch deepened the kiss. His arms tightened around her narrow waist. Her breasts pressed against his chest. Every nerve in her body tingled. It would be so simple to invite him in, take him to her room and let him make love to her all night.

He wasn't making promises and she wasn't asking for any. They were adults. No big deal. Yet, deep inside her, a tiny and much-too-reasonable voice shouted, *Very, very big deal.*

He pulled back from the kiss but kept his arm wrapped around her. "You taste so good."

"So do you."

His eyes darkened. "I want you, Kelsey." Reason clawed through the desire and shouted, *Run for your life!*

She leaned her forehead forward, resting it on his shoulder. "This is a mistake, Mitch."

He stroked her hair with his hand. "It doesn't feel like one to me."

She drew in a deep breath. "I can't."

For a long moment, he said nothing. Then he kissed her on the forehead and stepped back. "I'll swing by tomorrow morning and see if you found anything in the attic."

Already, she missed his warmth. "Okay."

She opened the front door and walked inside. Through the screen door she watched him go to his car. The interior light of the car clicked on when he opened the door. For a moment, he turned toward her and their gazes locked. He sighed and closed the door. The light was gone and his body vanished into the shadows. He started the engine and drove off.

For the second time in her life, Kelsey was tempted to put down roots. She wondered what it would be like to see Mitch every day and to make love to him every night. A smile curved the edges of her lips.

She shook off the floaty sensation.

Life had taught her so many hard lessons. She'd learned long ago that dreams were dangerous and led to pain. She had the here and now and that was it. She'd be wise to remember that.

She sighed. The sooner she got out of this town, the better.

Kelsey closed the front door. Moonlight streamed through the windows, casting tall dark shadows on the long hallway.

A sudden, overwhelming sense of worry washed over her. Nothing was out of place, but the house felt *different*. Had someone been in here? Or were her overstimulated nerves going haywire?

"I've got a gun!" Kelsey shouted. She didn't have one.

An eerie silence answered her. Her heart thundered in her chest as she flipped on the light. She half expected to see someone standing in a darkened corner. No one was there. The light banished some of her worries and she felt foolish. She slowly ventured farther into the house.

She pulled out her cell phone, ready to call 911 if need be. Then she realized the battery was dead—drained from telling the children's fortunes with the Mystic I Ching game on her phone. Damn.

"I've got the police department on speed-dial," she said in a clear voice. Silence. "Mitch Garrett can be here in minutes to whup your ass. So if you are here, get lost."

A mouse scrambled in a distant dark corner. She jumped. When she realized it was a rodent and not a person, she felt foolish. "And I'm buying big mousetraps first thing in the morning."

She considered calling Mitch from the land line, but decided against it. A: she was pretty sure now that this was not an emergency. And B: the last thing she needed to do was invite Mitch into her house. She knew after he searched the house, she'd end up in bed with him. And that was not going to happen.

Kelsey stood in the entryway for several minutes. She was glad now she'd replaced Ruth's sixty-watt bulbs with one-hundreds. However, the trade-off was that she couldn't turn on more than five lights sharing a circuit at one time or she'd blow a fuse.

"Coming upstairs," she shouted. "Gun in hand, finger on 911." Nothing.

Her nerves relaxed and by the time she'd reached the top of the stairs, she was feeling really foolish. She turned the lights on upstairs and went to her room. She closed and locked the door behind her, plugged her cell phone into the charger and set it on the nightstand. She opened her window to let the fresh air into the room. She was on the second floor and decided only Spider-Man could climb the north face of the house.

She changed into the oversized black T-shirt that she always wore to bed, washed her face and brushed her teeth.

By the time she'd climbed into bed, the surge of adrenaline had drained away and exhaustion had turned her limbs to mush.

She shut off the light at her bedside table and lay in the dark. She surrendered to fatigue and closed her eyes. Her muscles relaxed. And her mind drifted back to the evening she'd spent with Mitch. It had been so nice.

A car door slammed closed. By the sound of it, the car was parked directly across the street.

Kelsey sat up in bed, fully awake. Her heart thundering against her ribs, she hurried across the cold wood floor to the window.

A streetlamp shone down on the dark car. Inside was a figure clad in black. The driver glanced up toward her window as if knowing she'd be watching, raised a gloved hand and waved before driving off.

# Chapter 11

Nighttime had a way of exaggerating fear. Kelsey knew this from experience. Anyone could have been in that car, including Mrs. Baugh across the street or Mr. Wellington from next door. And though she thought the driver had waved to her, she couldn't be certain.

Despite all the reasoning, Kelsey didn't fall asleep until very, very late last night. Waiting and listening, she'd lain in bed, cell phone in hand, until almost three in the morning.

Now this morning, at ten past nine, Kelsey's eyes itched and her muscles ached as she pulled down the steps to the attic.

She glanced up the darkened stairs. The attic was the last place she wanted to go, but she suspected if there was any clue to Donna's past, it was up there.

She rechecked her fully charged cell, which she'd clipped to her cut-off jeans, and then climbed the stairs. A spider web brushed her face and she viciously swiped it away. The web clung to her skin and hair. God, she hated spiders!

With one foot remaining on the pull-down steps, she took a deep breath. "Don't be such a baby, Kelsey," she muttered. She climbed the last step. Searching for the light cord, she stood and immediately bumped her head on the rafter.

"*I hate this. I hate this. I hate this*," she said as she rubbed the tender spot on her head. She found the light and clicked it on.

The attic was filled with boxes and unused furniture, but it wasn't nearly as bad as she'd first thought. No doubt the climb up here was too much for Ruth in recent years, which was why she'd chosen to hoard her papers downstairs.

Kelsey blew the dust off a brown cardboard box and opened it. Inside were children's clothes. She lifted a faded red smock dress and wondered whom it had belonged to. There was nothing written on the box to indicate this. She replaced the smock in the box. There had to be fifty different boxes and trunks up here.

She started down the stairs with the first box. This was going to be a long day.

By midday, the upstairs hallway was filled with a dozen boxes. She'd gone through them all and so far had found nothing.

As she squatted in front of a hat box filled with parking ticket stubs, her cell rang and she glanced down at the number on the display. She recognized the number of Grant's Forge's Sheriff's Office—Mitch. Memories of the kiss they'd shared warmed her skin. She'd not expected to talk to him so soon. She was getting too close.

She let the phone ring until her voice mail picked it up. *1 Missed Call* blinked on her screen. She silenced the ringer and clipped the phone back to her waistband.

By five o'clock, the front hallway was filled with boxes from the attic. She'd found some treasures—pictures of people she didn't know in a shoe box, a dried and withered wedding bouquet in a hatbox and warped records that dated back fifty years. Only a few boxes remained in the attic, along with an extra large steamer trunk that was too cumbersome for her to move alone. To add to her frustration, the trunk was locked.

Kelsey swiped the sweat from her forehead as she set down a box. Dirt streaked her white T-shirt and strands of blond hair had slipped free of her ponytail.

The front doorbell rang, and she hesitated. After the doll and a possible late-night visitor, she wasn't so anxious to open the door. She moved to the top of the stairs.

"Kelsey! It's me, Mitch."

She pressed her palms to her cheeks. Oh, great.

He pounded on the door. She sensed if she didn't answer, he'd send the Marines in next. "Coming."

She smoothed the wisps of hair back off her face and opened the door. Mitch stood on the doorstep dressed in faded jeans, a gray T-shirt and running shoes. He held a large paper bag in his hand that smelled of Mexican takeout. From behind his aviators, he glared down at her. "What happened to you?"

The concern in his voice caught her off guard. "I've been up in the attic all day."

"Ever think to answer your phone?"

"I silenced the ringer." She glanced down at her phone. 5 *Missed Calls* blinked back at her now. Six forty-two p.m. "Sorry."

His gaze traveled past her into the hall. "Mind if I come in?"

"The place is a wreck." She stepped back from the door to give him a better view of the hallway.

"Looks like I came just in time." He held up the bag. "I bet you haven't eaten all day."

Again her stomach grumbled on cue. "I've been busy." She stepped aside and let him in. "Why is it you are always feeding me?"

"Have you eaten today?"

"No."

"Someone's got to look after you since you won't do it yourself."

She let the loaded comment pass.

His gaze traveled over the boxes and then to her grimy jeans and T-shirt. Vivid blue eyes lingered an extra beat on a scrape on her knee that she'd gotten when she'd slipped on the attic steps earlier.

Nervously, she tucked a hand in her jeans pocket. "The food smells good."

He cleared his throat. "Let's grab forks and a couple of plates."

Grateful for the task, she hurried to the kitchen and grabbed utensils and paper napkins. She washed her hands. "Why don't we sit on the back porch? I think I've inhaled a pound of dust today and could use the fresh air," she said. And inside the house his presence seemed to take over a room.

He followed her into the kitchen. "Sounds good."

She opened the back door and the two went outside and sat on the back porch step. The heat of the day had passed, but the sky remained crystal blue.

Mitch opened the bag, pulled out six different aluminum food containers and two sodas. "I got a little of everything because I didn't know what you'd like to eat."

She chose the taco salad with chicken and poured some salsa on it. "It all smells great."

He ladled an enchilada onto his plate. For a moment, neither spoke as they ate.

"So, you find anything interesting in the attic?"

"More junk." She took a sip of soda. "But there is a trunk I saw. It'll take a couple of men to bring it down and it's locked."

"I can help you with the lock tonight. Later, I'll get one of my brothers and we'll get it down for you."

"I'd appreciate the help with the lock. I have to admit, I'm dying to see what's inside."

"So how are you faring in the house? There are a lot of memories here."

"The memories I can handle, it's the other stuff that gets a little creepy."

"Other stuff?"

She had his full attention and now regretted her complaint. But there was no getting around it now. "Yesterday, someone left a Kewpie doll on my front porch." She sighed, chilled by the memory. "Its eyes had been scratched out."

"Why didn't you tell me?" Frustration coated each word.

"I didn't want to spoil anyone's day. And I didn't want to give whoever left it the satisfaction of ruining my day."

He set his plate down. "Any other problems?"

"Not exactly problems."

He leaned toward her. "Then what exactly?"

"I got a little creeped out last night when I was in the house. I got the feeling someone had been here."

He shoved out a breath as if he were trying to keep a rein on his temper. "Why didn't you call me?"

"I figured it was my imagination." Now with him here, her fears did seem distant and foolish.

"Anything else?"

"Right after I turned out the lights, I heard someone get into a car and drive off."

"You should have called me," he said tightly.

Her appetite gone, she set her fork down. Dependence on him was the last thing she needed. "I've been taking care of myself for years. I think I can handle a case of the jitters and a car driving off."

His jaw tightened and released. "I don't like this."

"It's just pranks. I saw my share when I was in high school."

"I've got two dead bodies and a missing man. Everything is suspicious until I prove otherwise." He started to repack the food boxes in the bag. "Let's get this in the refrigerator and have a look at the lock on the trunk. Then I'm checking you into a hotel."

"No one's chasing me off," she said.

He stood. "We'll talk about this after we have a look at the trunk."

Outside, a lone figure sat in an old pickup truck parked down the street from Kelsey's house. The driver had arrived just as Mitch had disappeared into the house. Mitch Garrett was an unplanned complication. But then life had been a series of complications since Stu had decided to open the quarry. The old bastard was quicker than first thought. A second slower and he'd have been dead and this whole mess would have been avoided.

The driver tightened gloved hands on the steering wheel. There were a good many messes to handle, but none was unmanageable. It was important to stay focused on the list of problems and deal with them one by one.

Donna had been a lying slut and anyone could have killed her. Chris was no longer a problem.

The second body found in the quarry had been in the water five years. Chances were very slim it could ever be linked to Donna.

And Kelsey, well, she'd been given warnings that she'd chosen to ignore. Now it was time to close the hymn book on her once and for all.

The driver climbed out of the car and strolled toward Ruth Warren's house. Kelsey and Mitch passed by the front windows and went up the stairs. They were headed back to the attic where Kelsey had been all day.

A gas can in hand, the driver opened the back door with a spare key copied from the key left under the pot and listened as they climbed the steps. Perfect. Killing two birds with one stone.

Glancing briefly at the boxes in the hallway, the driver went through the kitchen and down to the basement toward a pile of papers and spread gasoline all over them. The driver struck a match and tossed it on the gas.

Flames exploded, devouring the papers.

Within ten minutes, the house would be in flames.

Smoke was already filling the basement when the driver climbed the stairs. The driver moved to the front door, turned the key in the dead bolt and left through the kitchen, now filling with smoke.

Mitch bumped his head on the rafter. "Damn!"

Kelsey switched the light on. "I've hit it a couple of times myself today."

He rubbed his head. "No problem."

"The trunk is here."

Mitch pulled a penknife out of his pocket and crouched in front of the lock. Within seconds, it clicked open.

"Mighty fancy burglary skills, Sheriff," Kelsey teased.

He grinned as he flipped the trunk open. "I'm a jack-of-all-trades, baby."

The grin on his face completely transformed him. Hard features suddenly looked boyish and playful. She remembered the man she'd loved eight years ago. In those days, she'd stay awake at night just thinking about him.

With an effort, she focused on the contents of the trunk. The first thing to catch her eyes was a pile of yellowed letters tied with faded red ribbons. She picked up the stack. "The letters are addressed to Donna Warren. There is no postmark or return address."

Mitch dug through the contents and found a cheerleader uniform neatly folded. "Donna cheered for the high school."

"I don't think it was for long. She got into some kind of trouble with one of the coaches."

"Like what?"

"I think she slept with him."

"O-Okay." He pulled out a yearbook next and thumbed through the pages. He found Donna with the junior class. Mitch shook his head. "It always throws me when I see a picture of your mother. Except for the eyes, you are a dead ringer for her."

Kelsey peered over his shoulder. It was as if she were looking at herself. A cold chill snaked down her spine. "I've never seen a picture of her that young."

He handed her the book. "Pretty amazing."

"She looked very different by the time I was fifteen. She'd lost a lot of weight, her hair was shorter, brittle, and there were wrinkles around her eyes."

"Hard living."

Kelsey flipped through the book, looking for other pictures of Donna. She found her with the cheerleaders, but Donna appeared in no other group shots. When Kelsey reached the last page, a letter fluttered out. She picked up the envelope.

"What's that?" Mitch said.

"I'm not sure," she said opening the envelope.

Inside was some kind of official document. She unfolded it and inside was a Certificate of Birth.

"It's my birth certificate!"

Kelsey skimmed the names. "Mother: Donna Warren. Father: Unknown. No surprises there." Despite her easy tone, she had to fight off disappointment. She'd always hoped one day she'd find her father. She read on. "Place of Birth: Richmond, Virginia. Says here I was born at the Medical College of Virginia."

Mitch rested his hand on his knee. "A state hospital."

"Donna never had medical insurance."

"I wonder who covered the bill?"

"My father, maybe."

"A good possibility. Let's get some of this stuff downstairs where the lighting is better. I'd like to read through those letters."

Kelsey started to root through the box. "There's a letter here from a Richmond attorney. William Cranston. 701 Main Street, Richmond." The postmark was dated just weeks before her birth. She opened the letter. The reference line said Pending Adoption.

Mitch froze. "Do you smell smoke?"

Kelsey sat back on her heels. She inhaled. "I think I do."

"Let's get out of here."

"What about all this stuff? If the house is on fire, we'll lose it."

He wrapped his hand around her arm and started pushing her toward the attic stairs. "Better it than us."

Kelsey held on to the sides of the ladder and climbed out of the attic. Fingers of smoke reached up the center staircase.

She tamped down cold panic. "The smoke is coming up the stairs!"

Mitch was right behind her, taking the steps three at a time. "Let's get out of here."

He grabbed her by the arm and pulled her close to his side. They started toward the stairs. Kelsey's heart pounded against her chest. She leaned into Mitch.

Halfway down the stairs, the smoke thickened. From the belly of the house, the fire roared like a great hungry beast. The floorboards creaked and groaned.

Kelsey coughed and covered her mouth with her hand. Mitch tightened his hold on her as they reached the bottom step and hurried toward the front door. He turned the handle and pulled.

The door was locked.

Kelsey rubbed her stinging eyes. "It shouldn't be locked. I never throw the dead bolt."

Wasting no time, Mitch took Kelsey into the front parlor to the right off the entryway to a set of tall floor-to-ceiling windows. He tried to open one. It didn't budge. The windows had long been painted shut.

The fire's heat and thickening smoke made breathing difficult. Kelsey shoved a trembling hand through her hair. The house was disintegrating under their feet and would be gone in just minutes.

Mitch picked up an old Chippendale chair and threw it through the window, smashing the windowpanes. He yanked the curtain down, draped it over his arm and broke out the bits of jagged glass. Tossing the curtain aside, he took her by the arm and together they stepped onto the front porch.

She was aware of distant sirens as they ran down the porch steps and across the lawn. Only when they reached the other side of the street did she suck in a lungful of fresh air. She dropped to her knees, coughing.

Mitch came down beside her. He pulled in several deep breaths. "Are you all right?"

"Yes," she said. Her lungs still ached.

From across the street, Kelsey could see the fire through the first-floor windows of the house. The blaze had consumed the downstairs and had snaked up the stairs. A first-floor windowpane exploded from the heat.

"It happened so fast," she said, her gaze mesmerized by the flames.

Mitch stood and helped her to her feet. "Most fires move fast."

She noticed a spray of cuts across his forearm. Blood trickled down his arm over his hand. "You're cut."

He glanced down at his arm. "Yeah."

The sirens grew louder and within seconds two ladder trucks raced around the corner and down Ruth's street. No one said anything as the trucks parked and firemen went to work. Minutes later, a steady stream of water pummeled the house. The flames hissed and spit.

The fire chief came up to Mitch. "Sheriff."

Mitch nodded. "Walt."

"What do you think caused it?" the chief asked.

"I don't know. We were up in the attic and the fire seemed to explode around us."

"Mitch needs a paramedic," Kelsey said. "He cut his arm breaking a window so we could get out."

Walt nodded. "Let's get you both over to the medic. I want him to look you both over."

Kelsey fell into step beside Mitch. The adrenaline had vanished. Her legs felt like rubber and her head swam. By the time they reached the back of the rescue truck, she feared she'd collapse.

Mitch glanced down at her. "You're as white as a ghost."

"I'm okay," she lied.

Immediately, he cupped his hand under her elbow and guided her toward the truck. She sat down on the back bumper. A medic took one look at her, pressed an oxygen mask to her face and wrapped a blood pressure cuff around her arm.

Slowly her head began to clear. Mitch sat beside her, an oxygen mask on his face as the medic started to bandage his arm.

"You're not going to need stitches, Sheriff," the medic said.

"Good," Mitch said.

The medic's news eased Kelsey's mind and allowed her to shift her focus to the house. The firemen's hoses had doused the basement-level fire but the second floor and attic still burned. The attic filled with all those papers would be lost.

Sadness tightened around her heart. She yanked off her mask. "For years, I've told myself I didn't care about Donna, her past or even who my father was. It wasn't until tonight that I realized I was kidding myself. There are so many unanswered questions about Donna and the answers were right at my fingertips."

Mitch pulled off his mask and wrapped his soot-covered hand over hers. "It's not over yet, Kelsey."

The warmth of his hand seeped into her. "Everything is lost!"

"Now is not the time to talk about it," he said. "Let's get you out of here."

"Everything I owned was in the house. My wallet, my camera, my clothes." Her hand slid to her waistband where her cell phone remained clipped. She shook her head, smiling at the irony.

"What's so funny?"

"Figures my cell phone would make it out. My friends have always given me grief about my phone because I'm never without it."

He leaned toward her so that his shoulder brushed hers. "There's nothing wrong with that."

Tears filled her eyes as she stared up at the dying flames. "You know why I've always had a phone?"

His thumb rubbed the inside of her palm as he stared down at her. "Why?"

"So Donna could reach me. I always figured if I had a phone, she could find me." A tear escaped down her cheek and she swiped it away. "Dumb, huh?"

"Not at all." He rose and pulled her with him. "Let's get out of here."

"Where are we going?"

"To my place."

# Chapter 12

Kelsey laid her head back against the seat of Mitch's car and closed her eyes. She was vaguely aware of the ride over to Mitch's house, but couldn't tell what streets he took. Her mind was numb, and an overwhelming sense of exhaustion overtook her.

"We're here," he said, shutting off the engine.

Her head snapped up. She'd drifted off to sleep. "Where are we?"

"My house." He opened his door and the dome light came on.

She squinted against the brightness. Her vision cleared. He leaned toward her, one hand resting on the steering wheel and one on the seat. His presence filled the cab. As she looked into his eyes, she found a softness there that touched her heart. It would be so easy to lose herself in him. So dangerous.

Back at Ruth's, she'd not questioned the decision to come to his house—she'd only wanted to get away from the fire trucks and the ruins of Ruth's house. "Maybe this isn't such a good idea. I can stay at a motel."

"We'll talk about that in the morning. Right now, you need a hot shower and a good night's sleep." He got out of the car and came around to her door. He opened it.

She climbed out and stared up at the white two-story Victorian. The house was huge by most standards but the idea of sharing it with him made it seem very, very small. "This is your house?"

"I've been restoring it for the last couple of years. The first and third floors are still rough, but the second floor is done." Then, as if reading her thoughts, he said, "Five separate bedrooms."

He led her up the stairs to the massive front door, painted in black lacquer, and opened it. Inside the entryway, he turned on the light. The first floor looked like a construction zone. Tarps, paint cans and ladders littered it.

"It gets better," he said.

He guided her up the wide, well-lit hallway to the second floor. The upstairs hallway was painted in a pale yellow, the wood trim a glossy white. The wood floors had been sanded and varnished. The faint smell of paint hung in the air. She could see his attention to detail in the crisp lines of the dentil molding above and the gleam in the hardwood floors. The restoration was a labor of love for him.

Mitch walked her to a door at the end of the hallway and opened it. He flipped on the light. The room had a large four-poster bed with a canopy. The bed had sheets and blankets on it, but the wood floors were bare. The windows had simple white shades, but no curtains.

"I've left the decorating to Mom," he said. "She said something about white iolite—whatever that is—and lots of pillows. For now, though, it's kinda bare."

"It's great."

"There's also a bath through that door." He crossed the room and switched on the light. "Again, no frills but it's completely refurbished with plenty of towels."

She didn't bother to look. "I'm sure it's perfect." She stared at the massive bed that dominated the room. "You live here alone?"

"Yep." He moved to the threshold and paused. "No need to be nervous."

"I'm not nervous," she said a little too quickly.

"Then that makes one of us."

His honesty tipped her off balance. She blushed and remained silent, fearing her voice would reveal her feelings.

"I guess I should be flattered." His hand lingered on the crystal door knob.

She cleared her throat. "What do you mean?"

His gaze locked on hers. "I can still get under your skin."

Her jaw dropped open and then she snapped it closed. "You do not."

"It's okay," he said. His voice sounded soft, seductive. "Because you still get under mine."

"*Still?*" A simple word that spoke volumes about their past relationship.

He shoved out a sigh. "I had a thing for you the first time I saw you in the dive shop."

It took real effort to keep the emotion out of her voice. "Back in the day, that's not the impression you left me with."

"When you said the *L* word, I got spooked. I was too young. I came by your house the next day looking for you, but you'd already taken off."

She'd never known that. She'd called Ruth two days after she'd left so that her aunt wouldn't worry. Her aunt had never mentioned that Mitch had come back. Her aunt's deliberate omission stoked her anger but she caught herself. She had to let go of the past or it would kill her. "We were both young."

Still, Mitch wasn't talking about the *L* word now and she was smart to remember that. She backed away. "It's been a long day."

He nodded. "See you in the morning. Sleep tight."

She closed the door and leaned against it. *Sleep tight.* What a joke.

Kelsey awoke to bright sunshine streaming into her room. Disoriented, she sat up in bed and pushed her hair off her face. She'd lived in so many places that she'd become accustomed to waking up and not knowing exactly where she was. The sensation no longer made her panic.

As expected, her mind cleared. Mitch's house. Remembering her location didn't make her feel comfortable. In fact, she felt edgy.

She rose and padded into the bathroom. She looked in the mirror and grimaced. Though she'd showered and washed her hair, the faint scent of smoke hung in the air. She sniffed her T-shirt. Smoke. She slipped on her pants, which also reeked of smoke.

The first order of business today would be to get to a bank and have funds from her account wired to her. With luck, she could figure out how to get her credit card reissued and could buy a few new clothes.

She opened her door and found a pile of clean clothes, a pair of tan sandals and toiletries. Mitch.

"Bless you."

Disappearing back into her bathroom, she showered again, taking extra time to scrub her skin and hair. By the time she emerged, she'd erased the smoky smell.

She examined the clothes Mitch had left for her. He'd chosen a pink sundress with matching sandals; a bra and panties. All still had the sales tags on them. He must have gone to the department store and gotten them early this morning. She smiled as she pictured him in the women's section buying a bra for her.

She dressed, amazed at how well everything fit, and combed her hair and brushed her teeth. Refreshed, she walked out into the hallway. The faint smell of coffee and bacon teased her nose and lured her to the steps.

Last night, she'd been too exhausted to really notice the house. Now as she moved down the stairs, she could see where the line of renovation stopped. The front rooms of the downstairs hadn't been touched. Mitch clearly didn't put a premium on entertaining.

She moved down the long center hallway toward the kitchen.

Like the upstairs, the kitchen was completely renovated. Sleek black appliances complemented gray countertops, a double stain-less-steel sink and a tile floor.

She found Mitch standing next to French doors that faced out onto a wooded backyard. He was talking on the phone. By the looks of his frown, the conversation wasn't going well. He caught sight of her and nodded.

"Let me know if you find out anything else," he said, clicking the phone off. His gaze traveled up and down her body surveying the dress and sandals. "You look nice."

She glanced down at the sundress. "Not exactly my style."

"Sorry. Mom went shopping this morning and that's what she came back with."

"Your mom shopped for me?" She was oddly touched by the news.

"She'd heard about the fire and called this morning. She'd offered and I didn't want to leave you alone."

"I appreciate the thought."

His eyes held hers a beat longer. "Coffee?"

"Yes. Yes. Yes."

He chuckled and moved to the cabinet by the coffeemaker. He pulled down a white mug from a mismatched collection of cups in the cupboard. He filled it and handed it to her. "As I remember, you take it black."

The coffee felt warm under her fingers. She sipped it, amazed at how good it tasted. "So who got you so riled on the phone?"

He hesitated, as if he wouldn't answer, and then thought better of it. "That was the fire chief on the phone. He was calling from your aunt's house."

"And?"

"The fire wasn't an accident. It was arson."

"What?"

"They found burn patterns around the fuse box in the base-ment and traces of accelerant—gasoline."

She felt sick. "Gasoline?"

125

"The fire was set while we were in the attic."

She felt light-headed. Mitch took hold of her coffee from her and guided her toward a kitchen chair. "I knew someone wanted me gone, but I never expected this."

The intensity in his eyes threw her off guard. It would be easy to believe he cared about her. She cleared her throat. "So, is there anything that might suggest who burned down Ruth's house?"

"None. There was no sign of forced entry and whoever did this was very meticulous and detail-oriented. They didn't leave any evidence."

"That explains why the front door was locked."

"Yep."

"Great. I've got an efficient killer after me."

Mitch stood. "We've only begun our investigation. Something else might show up."

"I'm not counting on it."

Kelsey rose and walked to the counter. She picked up her coffee and tried to concentrate on the taste. "Well, I'm not waiting around for this jerk to strike again."

He tensed. "What do you plan to do?"

"I'm going to Richmond."

"Fiji I'd have expected, but Richmond?"

"I'm going to try and track down my father. I'm going to start with the attorney Donna hired to handle my adoption."

"I only glanced at the letter. I don't know where he is."

"William Cranston. 701 Main Street," she said.

He looked impressed. "You remembered that?" She tapped the side of her head. "Mind like a steel trap."

He didn't smile. "You may have a name and address, Kelsey, but that doesn't mean this Cranston guy is going to be there."

She walked to his phone. "May I?"

He nodded.

She punched 411 and waited for the operator. "Richmond.

William Cranston. Main Street. He's an attorney." Seconds later, she had his phone number.

He waited until she hung up the phone. "It's been twenty-five years and he may not know anything."

"Where's the Mitch with the can-do attitude?"

"He's here. But he doesn't want you to get your hopes up."

She ignored the concern in his voice. "I have to try. The last ten years, I've done of good job of pretending that there weren't any problems or issues in my life. But I've got them in spades. I never stay in one place more than a couple of months and my friendships are surface at best. The time has come to face who Donna was and what secrets she had. I need to get on with my life."

"You've done a damn fine job of surviving and prevailing."

"Thanks." She didn't need Mitch's approval, but it was nice. "But I've got to find out more about my past, not only for my emotional well-being but for my physical one as well. Someone tried to kill us last night."

He stared at her a long moment. "Give me twenty minutes. I'll shower and change and we can go together."

"You don't have to do this."

"I know you can make the trip by yourself, but this is for me as much as you. Someone tried to kill me last night, too. I have a tendency to take that kind of stuff personally."

"It's only a day trip. I'll be back by supper and will report in to you."

"*We'll* be back by supper." He dropped his hands to her shoulders and pulled her close to him. The heat of his body mingled with his masculine scent. She stood frozen, unable to take her eyes off his. There'd been a time when her love for Mitch had kept her going through some of the darkest moments in her life.

"Mitch," she said, "why are you being so nice to me?"

"I care about you."

"You didn't before."

They both knew what she meant.

He traced circles on the bare skin of her shoulder with his thumb. Her pulse beat faster. Her heart slammed against her chest. "I cared."

"But it wasn't the same."

"Given the same situation today, I'd handle it very differently."

She felt herself melting. "It was no accident that I chose the other side of the world to live. Driving you from my mind and heart was a full-time job for a while. I can't go through that again."

"I'm not the kid I was."

So tempting. Still, she pulled back.

He smiled. "I'll be down and ready to go in twenty minutes."

Freshly showered, Mitch had changed into khakis and a white-collar shirt. He grabbed his wallet and headed downstairs. He'd hurried because he half expected Kelsey to take off without him. It was a ten-mile walk to town to her car, but he didn't put it past her. She had a stubborn streak in her wider than the Blue Ridge Mountains.

He grinned as he started down the steps. In truth, he wouldn't have her any other way. Her tenacity had been one of the things that had attracted him to her all those years ago. He remembered the day he'd first met her. She'd just turned eighteen and was overseeing the delivery of refilled air tanks Stu had needed for a big dive expedition. The delivery driver was giving Kelsey a hard time. He'd expected Stu to be at the store and he'd refused to deal with a kid. She stood toe to toe with the six-foot-plus man, threatening to sue if he didn't release the tanks. The driver had laughed at her. Mitch had offered his assistance, but she'd told him to butt out.

Kelsey hadn't backed down. In fact, by the time she was done with the guy, he'd not only let her sign for the equipment but he'd apologized for questioning her.

Mitch walked into his kitchen and found Kelsey standing in front of the refrigerator. She was staring at her reflection. Her head turned lightly, an indication she'd heard him. "I feel like I belong on top of a cake."

He chuckled, amazed how quickly she could bury her emotions. "The stores in town won't open for a few hours but we can stop at one when we get to Richmond."

Grinning, she faced him. "Bless you. I also need to get money from the bank and another charger for my cell phone."

"Consider it done." He liked the way her face lit up when she smiled. If he had his way, they wouldn't go to Richmond but back upstairs. They'd spend the day in his bed making love.

He resisted the urge to speak his mind. "Let's get on the road."

"What about your job? Don't you have to work today?"

He snatched up his keys and cell phone. "The festival is over and the town's quiet. And I'd planned to take the day off anyway."

She waited on the porch as he locked the front door. "Some day off—you're tracking down leads that are over twenty-five years old."

He grinned. "I'd planned to sand floors in the third-floor hallway."

Kelsey laughed nervously. "If it were up to me, I'd sand the floors."

"The floors will be there tomorrow." He reached for her car door, but she made it to the door handle first. She opened her car door before he could reach it and climbed inside.

Independent. Stubborn. Bullheaded.

She drove him nuts.

He slid behind the wheel and started the car. She smelled fresh and clean—lemons. Her face looked pale and a bit drawn. She seemed tired as she tapped her fingers on her thigh. He knew Kelsey was more scared and nervous than she was letting on.

Ten years ago, he'd won her over without even trying. Now, wooing Kelsey wasn't going to be easy.

But good things were worth waiting for.

# Chapter 13

The ride to Richmond took forever. Searching for clues to her past would be unnerving on the best of days, but sitting so close to Mitch on top of it made her want to jump out of her skin.

Mitch had attempted conversation a couple of times. She offered curt answers, just too nervous to feign the nonchalance she used as a shield.

After they cleared Afton Mountain, he stopped trying to get her to talk. Silence settled around them. She let the monotonous line of trees along I-64 pass her in a blur of green.

"We're at the Gum Spring exit. Should be downtown in about a half-hour," Mitch said.

The deep timbre of his voice shocked her out of her haze. "I flew through Richmond when I came home. The place has grown a lot in the last eight years." He glanced at her. His gaze penetrated. "A lot's changed in eight years."

The attorney's office was located in a tall building at the corner of Main and Seventh Streets. The granite exterior looked as if it had once been white but now had faded to a dull gray. A long platinum light fixture hung above the number 701 secured atop revolving doors.

Kelsey's insides knotted as she stared up at the building. She tried to picture Donna, in her teens and pregnant, walking through these doors. Had she been as scared as Kelsey was now? Who had Donna chosen to adopt her? Why had her mother backed out of the adoption?

Mitch laid his hand on her shoulder. "You okay?"

No. "Yes. Let's check the directory inside."

Mitch guided her through the revolving doors and stood behind her as she stared up at the building directory. She scanned the alphabetical listing to the Cs. There were three Cranstons. One was an engineer, the second a real estate developer and the last a lawyer. Kelsey's mouth went dry. "He's here! Sixth floor."

Mitch shook his head. "Let's go up."

She took several deep breaths as Mitch pushed the elevator button. When the doors opened, she jumped. "I'm right here," Mitch said.

His deep, calm voice soothed fraying nerves. She'd never admit it, but she was glad he was here. She pushed the sixth-floor button.

The elevator doors opened and within seconds they found themselves standing in a small office at the end of the hallway. The receptionist, an older woman with graying hair, stood behind a large L-shaped desk. Her navy-blue dress was covered in dust. Around her were hundreds of case files piled high. The woman's sharp green gaze seared Kelsey and Mitch. She wasn't happy to see them.

"May I help you?" the receptionist said.

"I'm looking for an attorney named Cranston," Kelsey said.

The woman lifted an eyebrow. "What do you need?"

"He may have handled an adoption for my mother twenty-five years ago."

"Do you see this mess?" the woman said. "I've been sorting these files for two days. I can't tell you the status of today's case, let alone one that's twenty-five years old."

"What happened?" said Mitch.

131

The woman's sour expression softened when she looked at him. "Someone broke into the office three nights ago and tore the place apart. Files were scattered everywhere."

"Was anything taken?"

The authority in Mitch's voice had the woman sitting a little straighter. "Not that we've been able to see so far."

"Could we see Mr. Cranston?" Kelsey said.

The woman lifted a brow. "This isn't the best time."

"We won't take up much of his time," Mitch said. His smile belied the steel coating his words.

The woman chose not to argue with Mitch. She picked up her phone and cradled it against her ear. "Your name?"

"Kelsey Warren and Mitch Garrett," Kelsey said.

The receptionist buzzed an office down the hallway. She quickly announced their presence. The faint flicker of surprise sparked in her eyes. "He said to go on back."

Mitch guided Kelsey to the back office. They looked through the open door and found a man in his sixties standing and putting on his charcoal-gray suit jacket. His office, like the reception area was cluttered with files.

"Mr. Cranston?" Kelsey said.

He maneuvered around a long mahogany desk, his hand outstretched to her. "Pleasure to meet you . . . Miss Warren?"

His hand was cool, clammy. "Yes."

Mr. Cranston held her hand a beat longer as he stared at her face. "I'd offer you a seat but as you can see we are having some organizational issues."

"Your receptionist said you had a break-in?" Mitch said.

The attorney tore his gaze away from Kelsey and shifted his attention to Mitch. "We did."

Mitch held out his hand. "Sheriff Mitch Garrett." Cranston took it.

"Are you here officially?"

"Not yet."

Cranston dropped Mitch's hand and cleared the piles of files off the two chairs in front of his desk. He motioned for them to sit and then took his place behind his desk. "Nothing stolen that we could see, but I don't think I'll ever get this mess cleaned up. Mrs. Dixon, my secretary, is overwhelmed. Not very pleasant to be around right now." He sighed. "Nothing's been right since my secretary, Brenda Harris, quit. She'd have had it organized in no time. The woman never forgot a detail."

Kelsey tried to commiserate. "Maybe you could call her and she'd come in and help?"

"Believe me, I thought of that. But I haven't heard from her in five years. She just picked up one day and never came back. She *mailed* me her resignation. Didn't have the courtesy to tell me in person she was leaving. Twenty years together and all I get is a letter."

Mitch sighed, clearly frustrated that they'd veered from task. "This break-in of yours is too much of a coincidence for me."

"You lost me there," Mr. Cranston said.

"I had a fire at my house last night," Kelsey said. "Not only was the house destroyed, but I lost my mother's records and letters. I saw a letter from you in my mom's old yearbook. You had written to her about adoption. My mother was Donna Warren."

His eyes narrowed for a moment as he searched his memory. "I thought I'd seen you before when you came in. You look remarkably like your mother."

"Yes. Do you remember anything about the adoption?"

"Oh, yes. I surely do. It was quite a mess at the time."

"What happened?"

"I can't tell you very much. The adoptive parents were my clients. Their identity and anything we discussed is privileged."

Her heart sank. "Can you tell me anything? You said it was a mess. Why?"

"At the eleventh hour, your mother changed her mind."

"About the adoption?"

133

"Yes. She'd already received payment and just days before you were born, she demanded the adoptive parents pay her more money."

"She was selling me?" The words were out before she spoke them. Mitch laid his hand over hers. He squeezed gently.

Mr. Cranston sighed. "We call it compensation for lost wages and physical inconvenience."

"Physical inconvenience. That's what Donna's pregnancy had been," Kelsey said.

Mr. Cranston sighed. "Your mother was a . . . calculating woman. She always thought three steps ahead. When she raised the adoption fee, the adoptive father was angry. He refused to be blackmailed. Donna was furious. She stood right here in this office and threatened to disappear with the baby—you. Ironically, the next day the adoptive mother called me and said she'd pay the money. But by then, there was no trace of your mother." Perhaps she really had had second thoughts about keeping her.

She felt as if the wind had been knocked out of her. "Can you tell me anything else? Did Donna tell you who my father was?"

He stiffened slightly and stood. "There isn't much else I can tell you without violating my oath."

Mitch stood.

Frustration scraped over Kelsey's nerves. "There's got to be something else you can tell me."

The older man's eyes hardened with resolve. "There isn't."

She rose, knowing she'd hit a brick wall. "I could almost swear someone doesn't want me to find out about my past."

The attorney shrugged. "I'd like to help, but I can't."

"We appreciate your time," Mitch said.

"Maybe if we could find that old office manager of yours," Kelsey said. "She might know something."

"Good luck," Mr. Cranston said. "No one has seen her in five years. I received a postcard from her from Paris a couple of years ago. But I don't know where she is now."

Dead end. She glanced around at the piles of files.

One of them could hold the key to her past. So close and so very, very far away.


An hour later, Mitch pulled into the hamburger stand on Route 60. Mitch had chosen not to take the interstate, reasoning that Kelsey needed more time to collect herself. The attorney had given her just enough information to frustrate and upset her. They'd gone to the Department of Vital Statistics and gotten a copy of Kelsey's birth certificate. *Unknown* was written in the box for Father.

"What are we stopping here for?" she said.

"I could use a bite to eat. How about you?"

A faint smile touched her lips. "Still trying to feed me?"

"You're as thin as a rail and pale. And the half cup of coffee you had this morning won't hold you." He climbed out his side and closed the door before she could answer. He opened her door and together they crossed the gravel parking lot to the burger place. At the small window, he ordered a couple of burgers, fries and two milkshakes.

Kelsey leaned around him and said to the attendant, "Make my shake a water. And hold the burger on my burger. Just pile on the vegetables. Mustard, no mayo."

Mitch chuckled. "Don't tell me you are a vegetarian?"

"Vegan."

"You ate Dad's burger."

She shrugged. "I didn't want to be rude. It was so nice of him to include me."

It struck him that there was so much he didn't know about Kelsey and the woman she had become. What was her favorite color? Did she sleep on her right or left side?

"Your arteries will be weeping by the time you finish your meal," she teased as the cook dropped a burger on the hot grill.

"I'll take my chances." They stood outside the burger joint.

The sun was warm, the humidity low. It was a stunning day. "So when did you give up meat?"

"About six years ago." She met his assessing gaze. "No political statements. Eating meat just doesn't seem right for me."

"You're a soft touch, Warren."

"Say it again, and I'll punch you."

He laughed. The easy banter felt good. "I think we're having a normal conversation."

She laughed, banishing the shadows from her eyes. "It's got to be a first for us."

"It is."

The attendant called Mitch's number and he picked up their food. They sat on the picnic table by the shop and he doled out the meals. They ate in silence for several minutes.

"So what's our next step?" Kelsey said.

*Our.* He liked the sound of that. "Go back to Grant's Forge and see if the fire chief has anything he can tell us about the fire. And maybe LAPD and NYPD has gotten back with any arrest info they might have on Donna."

She sighed and set her half-eaten sandwich down. "We're not going to find anything on Donna, are we?"

He set down his shake. "I don't know. Someone out there is determined that we not find out anything about your past."

"They could make a mistake."

"That's what I'm counting on."

For the next several minutes, they ate until the silence was broken by the sound of puppies barking. Kelsey turned toward the sound. Off to their right, under the shade of an oak tree, sat a mother dog and five puppies. The black terrier-mix pups looked to be about ten weeks old. They were jumping around their mother, barking at her as she sauntered away from them. Tacked to the tree was a hand-painted sign that read Free.

Kelsey's eyes brightened. "I love puppies."

"Let's have a look at them."

136

She rose quickly and moved toward them. "Hey, fellows."

The puppies stopped and looked at her. Four of them hung back. Only one tumbled toward her, yelping and wagging its tail. The runt of the litter, this one had bowed legs and a bent ear.

Charmed, Kelsey dropped to her knees and held out her hands. The dog paused for a moment and then, wagging its tail again, came toward her. She scooped up the dog that wasn't much bigger than her cupped hands. The dog licked her face and nipped at her ear.

When the other pups saw Kelsey lavishing attention on their litter mate, they scurried over, not to be outdone. The puppies jumped on Kelsey.

Kelsey's deep throaty laugh had Mitch dropping down on a knee beside her. He'd never enjoyed a sight more in his life. If he could, he'd give all the puppies to her. She deserved happiness. "You should keep one."

She glanced up at him, hope in her eyes. "I really can't take care of an animal. I travel so much."

He shrugged. "If you really want something, you'd find a way."

She nuzzled the dog's nose. "I've always wanted a dog. Donna said they were too much work." The dog licked her. "But I bet I could keep you," she said to the dog. "You'd have to be a gypsy like me. But we could manage."

The dog yelped.

She laughed. "Well, then I'll take that as a yes." Cradling the dog close, she rose.

"Are you sure you want that dog? Don't you want to look at the others?"

"This pup fought to get my attention even when he didn't know what to expect from me. He wanted desperately to be chosen. I can relate to that." The pup licked her cheek. "So who do we talk to about this dog?"

*We.* He doubted she'd thought twice about the word. He did. "I'll take care of it." Mitch found out the pups were owned by the owner of the burger stand, who was more than happy to give the animal to Kelsey.

Fifteen minutes later, Mitch and Kelsey were back on the road, the dog nestled in an ice-cream-cone box filled with shredded newspapers.

"Thank you," Kelsey said.

He glanced at her. Lazily, she stroked the pup behind the ear. Sunlight streamed behind her head, highlighting her hair and adding a rosy glow to her cheeks. The utter look of joy in her eyes nearly stopped his heart. "You're welcome." He cleared his throat. "So have you thought about a name?"

"Buddy."

"Buddy?"

"I used to dream about having a dog when I was a kid. His name was Buddy."

"Buddy's a good name."

It took effort to keep the tightness out of his voice. Damn, but Kelsey was a survivor. There was so much to love about her.

*Love.* It certainly wasn't something he'd ever expected to find, but he had. He knew with utter certainty that he loved Kelsey.

The trick now was undoing the damage he'd done years ago and winning back her trust.

The ride home took longer because of Buddy. He'd needed several breaks. Kelsey fretted the first time she saw him squat by the roadside. "I thought boy dogs were supposed to raise their legs? Do you think that he is okay?"

Mitch smiled. "He's okay."

She tucked a strand of hair behind her ear. "I mean, if Buddy isn't the most masculine dog in the world, it's totally okay."

He laughed. It was a rich deep laugh that reverberated in her chest. "All male pups squat. He'll grow out of it."

He leaned against the car, his arms folded across his chest. With his legs crossed at the ankles, he looked so strong and powerful.

A warrior. He could be anywhere in the world, and yet he chose to stand guard over a couple of mutts.

She felt a sense of peace. "You've had a lot of dogs, I'll bet."

"My mother was a nurse before she married Dad. And for that reason she was dubbed the neighborhood savior of stray pets. Every pregnant stray or injured animal ended up at our house. We always had at least three cats and three dogs."

Buddy stood, wagged his tail and started to sniff the dirt, pulling her closer to the car. He found something of interest in the dirt and started to dig.

She stood less than a foot from Mitch. "That sounds great. You were a lucky kid, Garrett."

He hesitated and nodded. She could feel the tension tightening the muscles in his body.

She laid her hand on his forearm. "You don't have to do that."

"Do what?"

"Apologize for your great childhood. Mine was crappy but I've made peace with that. It's okay."

He took her hand in his. Warm, strong fingers wrapped around hers. Gently, he tugged her toward him. "If I could take all the pain away, I would."

Her lips, just inches from his, felt so dry. She moistened them. "Then you would change who I am. I like who I am."

His eyes softened. "So do I." He kissed her, pressing his lips gently against hers. He was testing to see if she'd balk. She knew one word from her and he'd back off.

Kelsey leaned into the kiss, vaguely aware that the dog yapped at her. Mitch tasted so good. What she wanted from him now had nothing to do with protection or security. She wanted him to make love to her.

He wrapped his arm around her waist. Her breasts flattened against his hard chest. Through her bodice, she could feel his rapid heartbeat thrumming against her skin.

Her body pulsed and demanded release. Her mind drifted to

the backseat of the Suburban. They were on the side of a rural road. No one would see them if they lay on the backseat.

Buddy barked and nudged his nose against her ankle. It took everything in her to break the kiss and glance down at the dog. He had wrapped his leash round their ankles and was hopelessly tangled.

Kelsey and Mitch laughed.

"Our timing is as impeccable as always," Mitch said.

She thought about the first time they'd made love. It had been in the back of the scuba shop, in the storeroom. "To say nothing of our choice of locations."

Mitch picked up Buddy, unfastened his leash and then unwound it. The dog licked his chin and Mitch ruffled him between the ears. "We better get back to Grant's Forge," he said, looking at the dog. "I've a nice spot in my garage you'll like."

Extreme focus kept her voice even. "We're coming back to your place?"

His gaze settled on hers. "Why not? I've got more space than I need and the motels won't take a pet." Buddy barked at her. "See? My man Buddy, here, is okay with the idea."

They both looked at her, waiting for an answer. She was playing with fire and she knew it. "Just for a few days."

"Until you get your business sorted."

"Exactly."

He grinned. "Exactly."

Mitch's two-car garage was military neat. Shelves filled with dozens of different tools and neatly labeled paint cans hung above a neat work bench. Extension cords, ropes and larger tools hung from a pegboard.

Kelsey settled Buddy in his garage bed with a rawhide bone. Mitch had found her a cardboard box and a couple of old blankets with which she'd lined the makeshift bed. She set out his new bowls and filled one with Puppy Chow and the other water. "Do you think he'll sleep?"

Mitch switched on a small clock radio on the work bench and tuned it to an easy listening station. "I think so. He's had a long day."

She hovered close to the dog's box, knowing once Buddy was asleep it would be just she and Mitch. "Do you think he needs another walk?"

"You've taken the dog out three times since we arrived." He laid his hand on her shoulder. Sexual energy ricocheted through her body. "Let's head upstairs."

"Okay."

# Chapter 14

Kelsey stood in the upstairs hallway facing Mitch. Though it was only eight o'clock, he'd locked up the downstairs and shut off the lights.

He took her hand in his and gently rubbed his thumb against her palm. Her heart thundered in her chest. The doors to his room and hers were open. Without words, she sensed again he was giving her a choice.

"You're not being fair," she said. Her voice was a hoarse whisper.

A slight smile tugged the edge of his mouth. "What do you mean?"

"You know when you touch me, I can't think."

He lifted an eyebrow, as he continued to make slow deliberate circles on her palm. "Really? I thought I'd lost my touch with you."

Heat rose in her body. "I wish you had."

"Why?"

"You throw me off balance and I don't like it."

He grinned. "Not even just a little?"

"I don't want to get hurt again." There, she'd said it.

He tugged her toward him and cupped her face. "I'd have done things differently the last time if I'd had a brain. This time won't be a replay of the last."

"How about we don't make any promises?"

He frowned.

But before he could speak and she lost her nerve, she rose up on tiptoes, wrapped her arms around his neck and kissed him. Immediately, he pulled her to him. The kiss deepened.

She wasn't sure how long they stood there. Time ceased to matter. The problems of the last week vanished. It was just the two of them.

Mitch ended the kiss, but he kept his hand on her arm as if he didn't want to break the connection. He guided her into his bedroom. Kelsey willingly followed.

A very large four-poster bed, crisply made with a tan coverlet, dominated the room. She was vaguely aware of a dresser, windows, a door leading to a master bath, but now it was the bed that held her attention. She sat down on it staring up at him. After kicking off her sandals, she scooted to the center. The pink sundress slid up her thighs.

His eyes darkened as he drank in the sight of her tan, taut legs. The mattress shifted as he came down on the bed and straddled her body.

He ran his hand up and down her smooth leg. "Silk," he whispered, his voice rougher than sandpaper.

She smoothed her hands down over his chest and tugged the ends of his shirt out from under his belted waistband. He pulled off his shirt and tossed it on the floor beside her sandals.

Dark hair covered his tan, muscled chest. His belly was flat, the muscles so defined they looked as if they had been carved from marble.

She slid her hand toward his belt and unfastened it. He sucked in his breath as if he'd been burned. At least she wasn't the only one ready to explode with desire.

Mitch lifted his hips so that she could push his pants down. She cupped his hard buttocks in her hands.

"Keep that up, and this will be over before it starts," he said.

"Quick and dirty works for me," she said.

"Sold."

"Do you have a condom?"

"Nightstand." He put on the condom in record time, though his hands trembled slightly as if he were a teenager. He pushed up Kelsey's dress and helped her wriggle out of her panties.

Sweat trickled between her breasts. She'd never wanted a man so much in all her life.

He pressed his erection against her moistness and then in one thrust pushed inside of her. Her body was so tight. It had been a very long time since Kelsey had been with a man. Sensing this, Mitch waited and let her body grow accustomed to him.

Soon he was moving inside her. His thrusts grew in intensity, mirroring her building desire. He lost himself to the erotic sensations. Within minutes, they both climaxed.

Mitch collapsed against her, dropping his head by her neck. His breathing was rapid, as if he'd just run a race.

Kelsey drew lazy circles on his bare back. She'd never felt more relaxed, more at peace. Finally, he rolled off her and onto his back. She yanked down her skirt.

"How about a shower?" he said.

Now that the passion had gone, Kelsey felt shy. "You go ahead."

He took her hand and pulled her off the bed. "Don't tell me you are nervous?"

She shrugged, unable to deny it.

"Darlin', after what we just shared, what's a little water among friends?"

She kept her gaze hooded, unreadable. "Friends? Is that what we are?" She treaded into dangerous waters.

Mitch was determined to keep it light as he guided her toward the bathroom. He didn't want to spook her with a lot of the sloppy emotional words she didn't seem to like. But he wasn't going to deny that they'd crossed a threshold.

"Figure of speech," he said easily. "I'd say we passed *friends* about ten minutes ago." He reached in the large glass shower stall and turned on the water. The water heated, and steam started to fill the room.

Mitch reached for the buttons that ran down the center of Kelsey's dress. He unfastened three. The creamy edge of her breasts peeked out. "I'm liking this dress more and more."

She lifted a seductive eyebrow. "What do you like about it?"

He reached inside the folds of the soft fabric and cupped her breasts. "This."

She arched back, pressing her breasts against his hands. He grew hard again. The steam wrapped around them. He unfastened the last of the buttons on her dress and slid the straps off her shoulders. It fell to the floor.

She reached for his erection. They'd just made love and already he was ready to explode again.

He wrapped his arms around her waist and lifted her out of her dress and then set her a few inches away from him. "Let's make this one last," he said.

She laughed and guided him into the shower. Hot water pelted their bodies. He pressed his erection against her naked flesh. Despite his hope to savor this moment, raw, animal need pulsed through his veins. He wanted to be inside her again. Now.

He plastered her body against the shower wall, grateful now he'd paid extra for the larger stall. She hitched a leg around his waist and he pushed inside of her again. Her breathing was ragged and her fingers bit into his back. She dropped her head back against the shower wall and moaned. Water beaded on her breasts and taut nipples.

Mitch couldn't take it anymore. Again, he started to drive faster and faster into her. She gripped his shoulders.

He exploded inside of her.

It didn't hit him until after the fact that he'd forgotten to put on a new condom. With Alexa or any other woman, he'd never made a mistake like this.

But the idea that Kelsey could be carrying his baby now didn't bother him in the least. In fact, it pleased him.

Later, Kelsey sat on the counter stool in the kitchen. Dressed in his oversized robe, her hair was still wet and her body thrummed with a delicious satisfaction. Mitch stood behind the counter, wearing only his jeans as he cracked a couple of eggs into a bowl. An omelet pan heated on the gas stove.

She pinched a bite of freshly grated mozzarella cheese. "And you cook, too. You are definitely a man after my heart."

He started to whisk the two eggs together. "That's the plan."

He spoke casually, but she sensed an underlying tension. Neither had spoken of tomorrows or the problems she'd yet to face.

"We forgot the condom during round two." The chances of a pregnancy now were slim to none and to her amazement, she felt a twinge of disappointment. The moment of sentimentality surprised her. She was practical to the bone when it came to this kind of thing.

"If you're worried about STDs, I'm clean." And there was that, too.

"So am I," she said.

"Then we've nothing to worry about except pregnancy."

She gulped. "We should be okay on that front, too."

His expression was unreadable. "Okay."

God, this was all too serious. "Where'd you learn to cook?" she said.

He shrugged, accepting the change of conversation in stride. "If a man wants to eat well, he learns to cook."

"In all honesty, I've only mastered a few dishes," Kelsey said.

He poured the eggs into the hot pan and they started to sizzle. "Stick around town for a while and I'll teach you a couple of new dishes."

After they ate, they made love again before they fell asleep in each others' arms. Kelsey had never felt so content, so at peace.

146

"Bitch!" A figure stood in the woods outside of Mitch's house and watched Kelsey pass in front of a window. The fire should have killed her.

The arsonist stared down at trembling hands and drew in a deep breath. Too many things were going wrong. Donna's body had been found. And then Brenda Harris's. Chris. The fire.

"This has got to end now." The arsonist heard laughter and whirled around to find Donna Warren standing just yards away.

Donna had not returned for his usual taunting in several years. And now here she stood, her hard eyes looking so much like Kelsey's, dancing with laughter. *"I told you I'd haunt you to your grave."*

The arsonist pressed trembling fists to an already pounding temple. The medicine was supposed to keep Donna away. "Get out of here!"

*"I'm a bad penny. I always turn up when you least expect it."*

"I won't let your brat ruin my life like you did. I won't!"

*"She'll finish you off. My daughter will avenge me."* The arsonist glanced up at Kelsey's window. This would end tomorrow.

"What have I done?" Kelsey uttered the next morning when she woke up and stared at Mitch's empty side of the bed. His pillow still held the crease from his head. The sheets on his side were still warm.

Grateful he wasn't there, she rolled onto her back and dug her hands through her hair. The heavy scent of steam from his bathroom still hung in the air.

"Kelsey, remember the one thing you weren't going to do when you came back to Grant's Forge?"

Damn.

Her body still tingled from his touch and his scent still clung to her skin. And she realized to her utter displeasure, she wanted to make love to him again. Double, double damn.

Maybe she'd have been more levelheaded last night if she'd not made that stupid vow of celibacy years ago. If she'd gotten around to sleeping with more men, any man, she wouldn't have been one big hormone waiting to explode. Her feelings for Mitch weren't special. They were strictly biochemical. She'd had an itch and he'd scratched it.

It wasn't Mitch she was responding to so much. She was primed for any man. Right?

Who was she kidding? She still had a thing for Mitch. "You are a glutton for punishment."

She remembered all those years ago when they'd made love and she'd poured her heart out to him. And he'd stared down at her as if she'd suddenly grown a third eye. Love was the last thing he'd expected or wanted then.

And it was the last thing she wanted now. Love was not on her agenda. Love was a bad, bad thing that only caused pain.

*Love.*

She sighed. God help her, she was still in love with Mitch Garrett. "Kelsey, you are so, so sad," she said to herself, feeling the need to leave.

She glanced around the sun-filled room, noticed that the light made the area look all the more spartan. There was a desk by the window, a chair and a bureau. The furniture was simple, but very well made. Mahogany.

She rolled out of bed. Her feet touched bare wood. No rugs to warm the floor. Naked, she searched for her clothes. She found her panties under the bed and her dress thrown over a chair.

She finished dressing seconds before Mitch appeared in the doorway. Barefooted, he wore faded jeans and a white T-shirt tucked in at his lean waist. He'd shaved and combed back his damp hair off his face. He held two steaming mugs of coffee in his hands.

The sight of him made her insides turn to jelly.

He grinned as he saw her fumble with the buttons between her breasts. "I thought you'd sleep late."

She managed a smile. "I've never been one to sleep late." She finished fastening the buttons and glanced down. She'd accidentally skipped the third button. Swallowing a few choice words, she unfastened the top five buttons and started to refasten them.

He set down the mugs on the desk across from the bed. "I can help you with that."

"No!" Kelsey didn't mean to shout the word but if Mitch touched her, she'd be right back in that bed before she knew it.

"Are you sure?" he teased. "I don't have to go to work. We could stay in bed all day."

She glanced toward the rumpled sheets on the bed and then back to his blue eyes, which had darkened with desire.

So tempting.

Kelsey shook her head. "I really should go and check on Buddy. I know he's got to need a walk by now."

"Already taken care of."

Why did he have to be so efficient? He moved a step toward her.

She retreated two. "Look, I really have to be getting back to town. I've got so much to do today."

He hesitated. "Like what?"

She dug her hands through her hair. "I've got to buy new clothes. I need a recharger for my cell phone. I never got one yesterday."

"All that can wait."

"No, it can't. I really need to get myself organized." She needed to get away from him!

His eyes narrowed. "What's wrong?"

Everything! "Nothing. I just need to get going."

"I thought after last night you might stick around for a while?"

She shrugged, trying to make the gesture look casual instead of stiff and jerky the way she felt. "I never stick around for very long."

"Kelsey, what we had last night was special." His voice had grown calm, steady as if he were talking to a jumper perched on the side of a building.

"It was great. Really great. No doubt about it. But let's not make it something it wasn't."

All traces of humor vanished from his face. His features hardened into granite. The loneliness that had stalked her for so many years squeezed her heart with a vengeance.

"Is this some kind of payback for eight years ago? Do you want me to feel the pain you felt then?" His voice was a low growl.

"No," she said genuinely surprised. "This has nothing to do with eight years ago."

"Oh, come on, Kelsey. It has everything to do with it."

"I just need to leave. There's no hidden agenda, no sick need to strike back."

"Then what is it?"

"I just need to get on with my life. I've got pictures to take, places to see." She wanted to sound a bit flip, but she sounded pathetic.

"You're full of it."

"Excuse me?"

"You're scared."

She narrowed her eyes. "I am not."

He moved a step closer to her. "You are running scared because for the first time in a long time you felt something."

"Don't confuse love with sexual satisfaction."

The edge of his lip curled up at the edge. "I've had enough sexual satisfaction in my life to know that last night was different. We have something special and I want you to stick around so we can find out what it is."

For a moment, her resolve softened. She wanted nothing more than to go to him and have him wrap his arms around her body. But she didn't. "I've seen too many men who'd declared their devotion to Donna and then, when the glow of sex faded, they took off."

"You are not Donna."

Unshed tears burned her throat. If she didn't get out of here soon, she'd lose it.

"Look, I don't need to be analyzed. I just need a ride to my car."

150

"Don't let your mother chase you away from the first bit of happiness you've had."

"My happiness is not dependent on you, Mitch Garrett. I'll have you know I've been plenty happy over the last eight years."

"You've been running so fast and so hard, you've never given yourself the chance to know whether you are happy or sad."

His words struck dangerously close to the truth. "Look, are you going to give Buddy and me a ride to town or do I have to call a cab?"

Frustration tightened every muscle in his body and he looked at her as if he wanted to shake sense into her. "All right. Ten minutes, downstairs." He strode out of the room.

She wrapped her arms around her chest and tipped her head back, trying to hold back the tears that now glistened in her eyes. One tear escaped and she savagely swiped it away.

"I am better off leaving. I am better off."

She silently chanted the words all the way into town as she sat next to Mitch in the front seat of his car. Buddy sat in her lap, content to sleep in her arms.

The wall between them seemed to grow thicker as they approached town. By the time they reached the scuba center, he reminded her of the cold, aloof sheriff that had pulled up at the quarry just a week ago.

One week. Had it only been only a week? She felt as if she'd lived a lifetime since then.

He put the car in Park. He walked around to the tailgate, opened it and removed the garbage bag full of Buddy's belongings. She climbed out of the car, holding the puppy close.

Mitch strode toward her and handed her the bag.

She reached for it.

He didn't let it loose. "Kelsey, this isn't over between us."

"Let's not go through this again."

"I'm not, right now. You're running scared and for now, I'll let you. But know that I am not giving up on us. What we have is too good to toss away."

151

Pain squeezed her heart. She opened her car door and summoned the nerve to look him in the eye. A steely resolve had replaced the anger.

And, in truth, it frightened her more.

She yanked the bag away. "Goodbye." She hurried into the scuba shop.

Mitch hesitated and then got into the car. He drove off, the wheels of his Suburban digging into the gravel.

The bells on the scuba shop door chimed over her head as she entered. She leaned against the glass door and squeezed her eyes tightly closed.

Buddy whimpered in her arms and glanced up at her. He licked her face.

She glared at the dog. "Don't you start with me, or I swear I'm going to crack."

# Chapter 15

Mitch gripped the steering wheel so tightly it was a miracle he didn't pull it off the steering column. Anger boiled inside him. Kelsey was being a damn fool. She was running scared and didn't have the sense of a gnat right now.

The last place he wanted to be now was his home where his sheets still smelled of Kelsey and their love-making. He turned right onto Main and headed to the office. So much for his day off. Pitiful.

He parked his car and strode inside. Mabel was sitting at her console.

She peered over her half glasses. "Don't tell me you volunteered to work today?"

"What's wrong with getting ahead?" His voice sounded harsher than he'd intended.

Mabel answered his surly manner with a look that had been perfected by mothers and teachers for thousands of years. "Don't bite my head off. You're the one that fell for Kelsey, not me."

"Don't tell me ESP is also one of your talents."

"It's a small town. More than a few folks saw the way you were mooning over that Warren girl at the picnic. And I hear you dropped her off at the scuba center this morning."

"I wasn't mooning. And mind your own business."

Mabel grinned. "*Lovesick puppy* was one of my favorite descriptions of you this morning."

Mitch muttered an oath. "This town is getting too small."

Before Mabel could answer, the dispatch radio buzzed. "Unit 26 to Dispatch. Unit 26 to Dispatch." "Dispatch here 26," she said.

"The canines have found a body off Route 702. You might want to give the sheriff a call. It looks like Chris Hensel. He was murdered. Shot in the chest."

Mitch expelled a breath. Damn. "What's their position?"

Mabel glanced up at him. "Sheriff is standing right here."

"A half-mile after 'The Flatlands' on the south side." The Flatlands was the police department's nickname for a flat stretch of land. They had renamed most of the landmarks along Route 702, which extended the length of the county, to allow for quicker location identification.

"I'll be there in ten minutes." He went back to his office, retrieved his spare .45. "Mabel, call the state police and alert the coroner's office. Tell them we have another body."

"This is all feeling a little too coincidental, Mitch. Do you think we have a serial killer?"

"I don't know what the hell we have. All I know is that it's related to that quarry and somehow to Kelsey."

"Kelsey? So far, I just see a connection to her mother's body. What do Chris and especially the other Jane Doe have to do with Kelsey?"

"The Jane Doe was shot in the chest, too."

"Yeah. So?"

"Have the medical examiner see if he can connect the Jane Doe to Brenda Harris."

"Who is Brenda Harris?"

Mitch couldn't explain his hunch, but his gut told him to react on it. "Call Bill Cranston in Richmond and he will give you the details. He's an attorney on Main Street."

* * *

Stu grinned when he came out of the back room and discovered that Kelsey was there. But when he glanced at her red-rimmed eyes first and then the dog who stared at him with one cocked ear, his smile vanished.

He shook his head. "I figured you and Mitch were a train wreck ready to happen when I saw the way you two looked at each other at the quarry last week."

Kelsey rolled her eyes. "What makes you think this has anything to do with Mitch? I've had a lot going on lately."

"Kelsey, I'm old, but I'm not blind or deaf."

She sighed. "He wants me to stay in town for a while."

"Horrible."

"He said he cares about me."

"The bastard."

"Would you stop making fun of me?"

He limped toward her. "I've every right to. You're acting like a crazy woman. You've got a fine man like Mitch who'd like to spend some time with you and you're running away."

"I'm not exactly running."

"You're running like a scared rabbit." He held up his hand to silence her protest. "I know you've had good reason to run before. Hell, I'd have run from this town, if I was you, but you don't have to run anymore."

She scratched Buddy between the ears. "Mitch and I have a history."

He sighed. "I knew there had been something between you two, but I never realized it was so serious."

The pain and humiliation from eight years ago rolled over her. "I fell in love with him almost from the first time I saw him all those years ago. But I made a mistake and told him that I loved him."

"What did he do?" A hint of anger had crept into Stu's voice.

"I still remember the look of shock on his face." She closed her eyes for a moment, trying to block out the image. She opened her eyes. "He tried to tell me that he cared about me and that he

155

wanted to be friends, but that was the last thing I wanted to hear after we'd just—" She stopped, too embarrassed to say.

Stu frowned. "If I'd have known that then, I'd have gone after that punk with a harpoon."

"Nothing happened that I didn't want. And I did give the impression that I had a certain amount of experience and I was just looking for kicks." But when she'd lain nestled in his arms that first time, the emotions had welled up inside her. All pretenses had melted away.

Stu let her talk.

"Looking back, I can see now why my words of love would have spooked him. I'd come across as some streetwise femme fatale and then I started spouting words of love." She sighed. "Talk about *Fatal Attraction*. He handled the whole situation as gracefully as possible."

"That's why you left town so suddenly that last summer."

"I needed to get away."

He sighed. "I didn't try to stop you because I knew you needed a fresh start. Ruth's house was not a happy place."

"No."

"Eight years is a long time. You're different. Mitch is different. Is a fresh start so bad?"

"It's very tempting and very frightening."

"No one said you had to marry the guy. What would it hurt to stick around for a couple of months?"

The dog started to wiggle in her arms and she set him down. "I'm supposed to be in Africa at the end of the summer to photograph leopards in Zimbabwe."

"You can fly out of Virginia as easily as the next place."

"Ruth's house is gone. I'm not sure where I could stay."

"Now you're grasping at straws. You know you can stay with me until you find a place and I'd bet Mitch wouldn't mind you bunking with him. The question is, do you have the guts to stick around and make a life here?"

156

A weight lifted from her shoulders. The worry melted away. "I could give it a try."

He grinned. "You sure could."

"I wasn't very nice to him this morning."

"Talk to him like you're talking to me and he'll get over it."

The bells on the front door of the shop jingled. "You've got a customer."

"Do you want a job here? I could use the help." The offer caught her up short. Accepting it would mean she really was going to stay for a while.

"Sure."

"Then it looks like *you've* got a customer. Give me the mutt and get to work."

She handed the dog's leash to Stu. "His name is Buddy. He might need a walk."

Buddy stared up at Stu, his large eyes looking especially pitiful. Stu shook his head. "Come on, you oversized rat. Let's go out back."

Kelsey grinned as she watched the two head out the back door. She smoothed her hands through her hair and headed to the front.

Sylvia Randall leaned over a display case, her manicured finger tapping softly against the glass. She looked up and smiled. "Miss Warren, how are you?"

Kelsey hesitated then smiled. "Quite well, thank you. Is there something I could help you with?"

She lifted a neatly plucked eyebrow. "You work here now?"

"For the summer. I thought I'd stay a while."

"Why, I think that is a fine idea. Summer is the best time in the Blue Ridge Mountains. Where do you hope to stay?"

"I haven't figured that out yet."

"Well, you are resourceful and I've no doubt you'll find something very quickly."

Kelsey's gaze dropped to the display case filled with dive computers. "Did you want to buy another dive computer?"

"Actually, I wanted to speak with Stu—or you—about diving lessons. My husband loves the sport and I'd like to be able to dive with him on our next vacation instead of sitting on shore and reading magazines."

"I've given lots of lessons before—it's how I first supported myself until my photography became popular."

"How wonderful." She leaned a little closer and dropped her voice a notch. "To be honest, I'd rather learn from a woman. I can't say I'm excited about squeezing into one of those skintight suits and parading around."

Kelsey glanced at the woman's trim figure. "I think you'll look just fine."

"You're kind." Her blue eyes sparked with excitement. "My husband is out of town today. Could it be possible for us to start our lessons today? We've a pool and all the privacy we'd need."

Kelsey hesitated. "I'll have to check with Stu on his lesson rates."

"I'm sure it's all very reasonable." A faint smile tugged at the edge of her lips. "How about we meet at my place in an hour? That should give you enough time to gather the equipment we'll need and meet me out at my house. You do know where it is, don't you?"

The Randalls' home was one of the largest in the county. Who didn't know where it was? "Out on Route 702?"

"Exactly."

"I'll see you in an hour."

"Excellent." Sylvia grinned. "This is so much easier than I'd ever imagined."

Uneasiness flooded her. As Sylvia walked out of the shop, Kelsey pushed her worries aside, rationalizing that her nerves came from the decision to stay in Grant's Forge. For the first time in eight years, she'd be staying in one place long enough to build relationships. She thought of Mitch and knew she owed him a big apology. As soon as she finished her dive lesson with Sylvia, she vowed to find him and make amends.

\* \* \*

158

Mitch watched the deputies load Chris's body into the coroner's wagon. His throat was tight with anger and sadness. Stu was going to be heartbroken. Chris and he had been friends for years.

Chris had been found off Route 702, about a half-mile into the woods. His body had been laid in a shallow grave and covered with a layer of dirt, sticks and twigs. A preliminary look at the body showed that he'd been shot through the chest, just as the other two bodies had been.

He'd never believed in coincidences. In his gut, he knew whoever had killed Donna and Jane Doe had killed Chris. Three murders, each one spanning a decade. And somehow they were all connected to Kelsey.

He went to his car and dialed her cell number. The phone rang once and went straight to voice mail, which meant it was off. Then he remembered they hadn't bought a charger for it yesterday. Likely the batteries were dead.

She might not want to see him face-to-face now, but he didn't give a damn. He wanted to check in with her and let her know what was going on. He had a bad feeling about all of this. As soon as he visited Stu at the dive shop, he was going to track down Kelsey.

A maid let Kelsey into the Randall home and escorted her back to the pool area. The older woman quickly excused herself and left Kelsey alone by the pool.

Kelsey stood by the Randalls' glistening stone pool, surrounded by lush gardens that blended seamlessly into the mountainside. In the distance, nestled in the valley below, was the town of Grant's Forge.

The Randall home was more stunning than she'd ever dreamed. When Kelsey had first gotten her driver's license, she'd driven by and looked at the house. She'd tried to imagine what it would be like to live in a place like this. In those days, she'd been certain that living in such a lavish home would have solved all her problems.

Footsteps sounded behind her and she turned. Sylvia Randall appeared wearing flawless makeup, white linen pants, a silk top and Bandolino sandals. She looked lovely, but not ready to dive.

Kelsey wondered briefly if she'd misunderstood the woman. "Did I make a mistake? Are we going to have a lesson today?"

"A lesson." Her eyes darkened. "Yes, we are going to have a lesson today."

"What you're wearing is very lovely, but you may want to change into a swimsuit before we begin."

Sylvia walked to a chaise, sat down and stretched out her feet on the white cushion. "I thought we'd take a few minutes to get to know each other."

Frustration welled inside of Kelsey. She'd run around like a crazy woman this last hour trying to get herself together. While Stu had rounded up the equipment, she'd run to the ATM to get cash and then to the department store to buy a swimsuit, shorts, sandals and a couple of towels for herself. She raced down Route 702 as if her hair were on fire so that she wouldn't be late. And now Sylvia wanted to talk.

Customers. She'd seen them all. And in all honesty, she'd had stranger requests from them before. She smiled. "What would you like to know? My dive qualifications?"

"Oh, I have no doubt you are qualified, Miss Warren. Stu wouldn't have hired you if you weren't. I want to know about you. You've had a very colorful life."

Her guard slammed into place. "Maybe."

Sylvia steepled her manicured fingers in front of her. "It must have been hard to find your mother in that quarry."

Kelsey drew in a breath. "Mrs. Randall, I'm happy to discuss my dive qualifications and the jobs I've had, but I don't discuss my mother."

Sylvia smiled. "Please, call me Sylvia. I'm sorry, dear. I can imagine it must be very hard for you. She wasn't the ideal mother."

Pride had her coming to Donna's defense. "How would you know what kind of mother Donna was?"

"Well, for starters, you call her Donna. When's the last time you called her Mom?"

"Never."

Sylvia shook her head. An odd sense of sadness and anger sparked in her eyes. She rose from the chaise. "I knew your mother *very well*."

Curiosity got the better of her. Despite all the trouble Donna had put her through, Kelsey still found herself hungry for information about her. "I can't imagine you two as friends. You said you knew her from the University Club."

"I did. And we weren't friends, exactly. Shortly after Boyd and I were married, your mother came to work for us as a maid." Her gaze bore into Kelsey. "It never ceases to amaze me how much you look like your mother."

"Yes, I've heard that often."

"No, I don't think you realize how remarkable the resemblance is. There are times when I feel as if I am talking to Donna." Sylvia's gaze locked on Kelsey, transfixed.

A tingle snaked down Kelsey's spine. This wasn't right. "Donna is dead."

Sylvia broke her stare. "Yes."

"Look, if you'd rather not have the lesson today, I understand. Maybe another time would be better." Maybe when hell froze over.

"No, no, don't go. I do want my lesson today. I've waited so long for it and I'd be quite disappointed if we couldn't have one." Sylvia seemed tense, anxious even.

This was too weird. "I think it's better you work with Stu." As Kelsey lifted the large rolling suitcase that she used to carry the equipment, Sylvia reached for a silver box on a glass table next to the chaise. The glint of metal in sunlight caught the corner of her eye and she glanced up.

Sylvia was holding a gun on her.

\* \* \*

Mitch dreaded breaking the news about Chris to Stu, but there was no avoiding it. He found Stu in the back of the dive shop. He'd half expected to find Kelsey at the shop, but to his disappointment, she wasn't there.

Stu glanced up from a regulator he was working on. "Hey, Mitch."

Mitch took off his hat. "Fixing a regulator?"

"Yeah, it always amazes me how rough divers can be with their equipment. The fellow that owned this one kept it in his attic for three years and now he wonders why it doesn't work. Hello, heat's hell on computers."

Mitch nodded, wishing there was some way to avoid what he needed to say. "I've got bad news."

Stu didn't glance up. "It's about Chris."

"We found him. He's dead."

He shoved out a sigh. "What happened?"

"He was shot."

Stu's jaw tightened. "Jesus, who would shoot Chris?"

"That's what I'm trying to find out."

Stu set the regular down. "He was the nicest guy. Never had an enemy."

"Did anything unusual happen that last day?"

"He borrowed a couple of hundred bucks from me, but that wasn't out of the ordinary. He was always strapped for cash."

"Why?"

"He liked to gamble. Nothing major, just a game of craps here and there."

"Could he have lost more than you realized?"

"Naw, he was always good about knowing his limits. And he always made good on his debts on payday." He frowned. "He did get a phone call a week or two ago. He was pale when he hung up. When I asked him about it, he laughed it off."

Mitch glanced around the shop. An overwhelming sense of unease settled in his bones. "Do you know where Kelsey is?"

Stu nodded. "She headed up to the Randall place. Sylvia wants to take dive lessons from Kelsey."

"I can't picture Sylvia getting her hair wet, let alone diving."

"I was as shocked as you were. I figured she'd walk a wide circle around Kelsey, considering her history."

"Her history?"

"Donna and Boyd had an affair years ago, before Kelsey was born. In fact, there was even talk that Boyd was Kelsey's father."

"Boyd told me about the affair, but he didn't mention the paternity issue."

"Despite Boyd's overactive libido, he adores Sylvia. When she threatened to leave him, he dropped Donna. I'm not sure how he fixed things between him and Sylvia, but he did. Donna left town and all was forgotten."

Kelsey looked so much like her mother. It made no sense that Sylvia would want to spend any time with her. And it had been his experience that women never forgot anything.

"You know Kelsey's staying for the summer," Stu said.

"What?"

"She wants to hang around for a while, see what develops."

His heart tightened. This was her way of giving them a chance. "I'm going to drive out there and check on Kelsey."

"She'll be back in a couple of hours."

His skin itched with worry. "No, I'm going now."

# Chapter 16

For a moment, Kelsey's mind didn't quite register the fact that Sylvia Randall was holding a gun on her. It was almost as if she were watching a television show. She could just switch the channel and the show would change.

But the show didn't change.

She struggled to keep her voice calm. "Sylvia, I don't understand."

"Don't you think the dumb blond act is getting a little old, *Donna*."

Kelsey drew in a breath. "I'm not Donna. I am *Kelsey*."

A faint smile curved the edge of her lips. "Right."

"Donna is dead."

"I know. I killed you. But you came back." A wave of panic washed over her. Sylvia was insane.

"You killed Donna. Why?" The words tumbled out of her with her breath.

"Please don't play me for a fool."

Kelsey's gaze dropped to the gun. She needed to stall for time. Perhaps if she could keep Sylvia talking, someone would find them, or she could edge close enough to get the gun. "I'm not. I'm just trying to understand."

Sylvia's eyes looked wild. "Understand? What's there to understand? You seduced my husband and then stole *my baby*?"

The seduction part didn't surprise Kelsey. Who hadn't Donna seduced? But the baby—that part she was almost afraid to ask about. "What baby?"

For a moment, Sylvia just stared at her, as if she were suddenly confused. Then she drew in a breath and her eyes seemed to clear. "Your mother never told you, did she?"

Sylvia was talking to *her* now and not Donna. "Tell me what?"

"Boyd and I wanted to adopt you. We wanted to give you all this," she said gesturing around the poolside with her gun. "We desperately wanted to love you and raise you as ours."

Donna had planned to give her up to the Randalls! The Richmond attorney had represented Boyd and Sylvia. "I never knew that."

"We'd had it all arranged." She sighed, her eyes wistful. "I had the loveliest nursery for you. It was yellow, with white clouds, and a hand-crafted crib from Italy."

"What happened?"

"Donna was a greedy bitch, that's what happened." Ice coated each word.

No surprise. "She wanted money for me," Kelsey said to understand.

"And we were willing to pay very handsomely for you. Money was no object for me. I wanted you so much I ached." A tear ran down Sylvia's cheek. "Just days before you were born, Donna went to the attorney and said she wanted double the money. And if we didn't pay, she threatened to disappear."

She knew what happened next, but she wanted to hear it from Sylvia. "What happened?"

"That idiot attorney contacted my husband first. Boyd was furious by the demand and refused to pay. Donna got angry and took off. When I found out I was heartbroken. I tried to find your mother and you, but she simply vanished."

There'd been times when Kelsey was a child that her mother would say she should have taken the money—that they both would have been better off. Kelsey had never understood. Now she did.

She drew in a deep breath. "Is Mr. Randall my father?"

"Boyd got your mother pregnant. She was so lovely in her day and he was taken with her. She knew it and used it to her advantage. I caught them in our bed. I still remember Donna's smug expression." The smile faded from her eyes as she relived that dark moment. "I adored Boyd and he rammed a knife in my heart. I threw him out of the house." She drew back her shoulders trying to collect herself. "He came crawling back several times, but I refused to see him. And then he came home offering the perfect peace offering. A baby."

"Me."

"Yes. Donna had told him she was pregnant and that the baby was his. For a price, she'd give us the baby." Tears glistened in her eyes. "We'd tried for five years to have a baby. Nothing worked. You have to understand, all I ever wanted to be was a mother. I'd dreamed of having four or five children. And I couldn't have *one*."

Kelsey willed her voice to remain calm. "Why did you kill Donna?"

Sylvia frowned. "Because she came back to town and demanded *more* money. Boyd was running for reelection to the state senate. That greedy bitch. She was determined to ruin us all over again. I couldn't let it happen. I had her meet me at the quarry. She had such a smug smile on her face." She straightened her shoulders. "I shot her while she sat in her car and then pushed it into the quarry."

Kelsey's head spun.

Sylvia nudged the gun toward the pool. "Get in the pool."

"You ran Stu over?"

"Yes."

Panic shot through her. "Why?"

166

"If he'd died, the quarry wouldn't have been opened and there'd have been no investigation." Her eyes narrowed. "Now get in the pool."

Kelsey glanced around looking for anything to use as a weapon. "Why?"

"Because you are going to drown today. It's going to be a terrible accident."

She took a step back. "You don't have to kill me. I can leave town."

"I told you to leave, but you didn't."

"You left the doll."

"Yes." Tears pooled in her eyes. "Did you know that doll cost me hundreds of dollars? I'd bought dozens for my baby girl. When my baby was stolen, I put them all in the attic. I couldn't bear to look at them."

Kelsey's heart ached for Sylvia. "Sylvia, please let me help you."

Her eyes sharpened and she swiped away a tear. "You think you can just hang around town humiliating me, whispering about Boyd's affair with Donna behind my back."

No matter how much she pitied Sylvia, the woman was dangerous. She glanced around for something she could use as a weapon. "I haven't said anything, I swear."

"You are a lying slut like your mother. You are just like Chris and the other woman. You all think you can bleed money out of me. Now get in the water!"

"I don't want your money."

"No, you took my daughter."

Sunlight glistened like diamonds on the crystal-clear pool water. Fear choked Kelsey. There had to be a way out of this.

Sylvia fired her gun.

The bullet grazed the side of Kelsey's arm and exploded into a potted plant behind her. Pain seared her arm. Warm blood trickled down her arm.

"Get in the pool!" Sylvia said.

"Someone is going to hear that gunshot," she said easing toward the pool.

"No one is here."

"That maid let me in."

"She's running an urgent errand in town for me. She won't be back until late."

Kelsey's heart sank. True panic started to settle in her bones. "People know I'm up here. If you shoot me, they will be suspicious."

"I got away with three other murders. And frankly I've gotten quite good at it."

"Who have you killed?"

"You, that stupid paralegal and that greedy diver Chris."

"Why them?"

"Both somehow figured out that I'd killed Donna. Both wanted to blackmail me." She sighed. "If there is one thing I hate, it's a blackmailer. No morals. No class." She nudged the point of the gun to the pool. "Get in."

The sound of the front door opening and closing echoed through the house. Kelsey's heart leaped with hope. "Help!" she shouted.

Sylvia glanced over her shoulder, her face hardened with panic.

Boyd came running out to the patio. He wore a white Izod and tennis shorts. His thick gray hair hung recklessly over his forehead. He was the image of a perfect father. She couldn't have dreamed of a father so perfect. He was going to save her when she needed him most.

His gaze darted between the two women. "Sylvia, what the devil is going on?"

"Mr. Randall, help me!" Kelsey said. "Your wife is trying to kill me."

He looked at Sylvia. "What is she talking about?" he said to his wife.

Sylvia looked relieved to see her husband. "Donna came back. I tried to get her to leave, but she wouldn't. Now I have to make her leave. Donna has to get in the pool and drown."

"Sylvia." His voice sounded so sad. "She's not Donna. She's Kelsey."

"She's Donna! Look at her. She hasn't changed a bit."

"Honey, you've got to listen to reason."

Kelsey's gaze darted between the husband and wife. She suspected he was the only one who could reach her.

"There's no reasoning anything anymore. She knows I killed the others."

Boyd tipped his head back, expelling a breath. "Why did you tell her?"

"Because she knows. Donna knows I killed her."

Boyd looked terribly sad and old as he stared at his wife. He knew she was insane. "I can't keep covering for you."

Tears spilled from Sylvia's eyes as she stared at her husband. Her mascara started to run down her cheeks, making her look all the more demonic. "This is the last time, Boyd. Please. Once she's gone, we will be done. There will be no others. We can leave town."

Kelsey cupped her hand over her throbbing shoulder. "Please, Mr. Randall, you've got to make her see reason."

"Shut up!" Sylvia shouted. "His loyalty is to his wife."

Blood trickled between Kelsey's fingers. "I'm *your* daughter."

Boyd's gaze darted between the two until finally it settled on her. "When Donna told me she was pregnant, I wasn't sure if the child was mine or not. I wasn't sure until you came back to town ten years ago. I came by the dive shop several times just to be sure. You looked so much like your mother, but you have my eyes."

Kelsey's heart ached. "Since I was a little girl, I've tried to picture my father." He swallowed.

Sylvia moved next to her husband. "Boyd, you've got to help me."

For several seconds he didn't say anything, his gaze locked on Kelsey.

Kelsey's arm throbbed and she needed to sit down. But she kept her gaze on Boyd. Her father. After all these years, he was going to save her.

He nodded. "I'll help you, Sylvia."

Sylvia smiled. "I love you, Boyd."

Kelsey felt as if she'd been punched in the gut. "I'm your child. Your flesh and blood."

He lifted his chin. "She is my wife. I've been with her for thirty years. I can't turn my back on her now. I don't know you." He moved toward her. "Now get in the pool."

Panic shot through her body like razor blades. "Go to hell!"

He winced.

Sylvia's smile looked smug. "Donna is just as crass as ever."

Boyd took the gun from Sylvia. He started to move toward Kelsey. Holding her ground, she glanced hurriedly back at the glistening cool waters. He meant to drown her. She curled up her fingers into fists. "You might kill me, you son of a bitch, but I won't make it easy for you."

With reflexes quicker than she'd anticipated, he grabbed her injured arm and squeezed. She screamed. She drew back her fisted hand and hit him in the side of the head. He yelped and backed away. Her hand throbbed as if she'd broken it.

Sylvia screeched and went to Boyd's side and helped him right himself. He leveled the gun.

"Shoot her!" Sylvia shouted.

A gunshot exploded.

Kelsey winced. For a brief instant, she thought she'd been shot. Then she saw Boyd drop to his knees. He'd been shot in the shoulder. Sylvia screamed and dropped to the ground with her husband.

Mitch stood by the door, his .9 mm Beretta drawn and ready to fire again. Tears welled in her eyes. She'd never been as glad to see anyone in her life.

Mitch didn't look at her. "Drop the gun, Randall."

His gaze was focused on Sylvia and Randall. Sylvia cradled her husband's head in her lap. His blood stained his shirt and her white pants.

Boyd released the gun and let it drop on the pavement.

Kelsey felt light-headed. She dropped to her knees. Her slight movement caught Mitch's attention and he glanced at her for a split second. Concern, fear and love reflected in his eyes.

In that second, Sylvia reacted. She picked up the gun and raised it toward Kelsey. "This isn't right," Sylvia wailed.

Mitch fired again, this time killing Sylvia.

Twenty minutes later, the ambulance and coroner had arrived. Boyd was weeping, calling out Sylvia's name as the deputies loaded her shrouded body into the hearse.

Mitch had barely spoken to Kelsey once he'd confirmed she was okay. She'd watched in shock as he'd cuffed Boyd and then tried to save Sylvia. He'd done CPR on her until the medics had arrived. There had been thousands of questions.

The paramedic had wrapped Kelsey's gash. She would need the wound irrigated and there'd be stitches, but she'd live. Exhausted, she lay back on the stretcher. The paramedics spoke calmly to her as they covered her body with a sheet and lifted her into the ambulance.

The paramedic climbed into the back of the ambulance with her and closed the door. He'd only been inside a split second when someone pounded on the back door. It was Mitch.

The paramedic surrendered his seat to Mitch and went to the front cab with the driver.

Mitch yanked off his glasses and sat beside her. He brushed her hair back with his calloused hand. "Are you all right?"

"Yes."

His fingers trembled. "Kelsey, I am so sorry about this. I should have put the pieces together sooner."

"This was the last thing I expected." A tear trickled down her cheek.

He wiped it away. "This isn't a good time for this, but I don't care. I love you."

The morphine had kicked in and she didn't trust herself. "What?"

He cupped her face in his hands and looked into her eyes. "I love you."

Out of all the insanity and pain came this one perfect moment. "I love you," Kelsey replied.

He kissed her on the forehead. "Stu says you're staying in town for a while."

"Yes. It's time I put down roots."

He kissed her on the lips. "You've saved me the trouble of chasing you around the world."

"You'd have left Grant's Forge for me?"

"Baby, where you go, I go. We're a team now."

172

**Keep reading for an excerpt from**
*Find You . . .*

# *Prologue*

Danger surrounded Elena Benito.

The dark sensation had grown steadily since she'd returned to Miami yesterday, winding her nerves tighter than a drum. At 9:00 a.m., just six hours from now, she was scheduled to testify against her brother, drug kingpin Antonio Benito.

Unable to sleep, Elena paced the small furnished room of the FBI's Dade County safe house. Feeling trapped, she sat on the twin bed, picked up the TV remote, clicked on the small television and started surfing. But none of the B-movies, late-night talk shows or infomercials distracted her from her fears. Her brother was out there, looking for her, and he wanted to punish her.

She clicked off the television. The house's old air-conditioning system couldn't overcome the hot, humid July air, making it difficult to breathe.

Rising, Elena flexed and released her fingers. She had to get out of this room.

She opened her bedroom door, which fed into the living room furnished with bamboo furniture and a green shag carpet. Flowery drapes covered a large picture window by the wooden front door.

175

This room felt as foreign as the safe house in New Mexico where the FBI had hidden her. Out west, she'd dreamed of getting out of the mountains and returning to the Miami she loved. She longed for her beloved beaches and the sight of the ocean. But now as she stared around this seedy house, she realized the Miami she'd loved was lost to her forever.

Police officers Jack Mendez and Nancy Rogers were the Miami officers assigned to guard Elena until the FBI detail picked her up at seven. The police officers' voices and the click of cards shuffling drifted out from the kitchen.

Both Rogers and Mendez had called this operation a routine gig, but there was nothing routine about any of this. The officers, like everyone else involved in her brother's murder trial, knew how much rode on her testimony. The Feds had been after Antonio for years. But they'd never been able to pin anything on him until Elena had told police she'd witnessed her brother kill six members of a local Miami church.

The "Churchmen," as they were known by the press, had effectively stopped the drug trade in their neighborhood with peaceful sit-ins and a neighborhood watch program. Angered by sagging profits, Antonio had decided to send all he knew a message by murdering the men. He'd forced Elena to witness the killings because she, too, was being taught a lesson: Never run from me again.

Elena had begged for the lives of the men, but Antonio had showed no mercy and shot each in cold blood. It had taken her another nineteen days before she'd found another opportunity to escape Antonio. This time, when she ran, she had gone to the police. She had identified her brother as the shooter and he had been arrested.

She moved silently through the house to the open kitchen door. Mendez stood at the kitchen sink as a coffeepot brewed. His white Guayabera shirt accentuated rich brown skin. "My old lady was talking about buying a bigger house."

Nancy sat at a yellow Formica kitchen table and shuffled a worn deck of cards. The room's pineapple wallpaper and appliances dated back to the fifties. "Her high-dollar tastes are gonna break you, Mendez."

Mendez's full mustache twitched when he smiled. "Nah, I can handle her."

Nancy dealt two hands. "That's what they all say."

Floorboards under Elena's feet squeaked as she crossed the threshold. Immediately the officers' gazes whipped around. Nancy was already reaching for her gun.

Elena rubbed smooth hands over designer jeans. "I'm sorry. I just wanted a glass of water."

Nancy clipped her gun back in the holster and smiled. "Sure."

"I'll get it," Mendez said.

As Mendez filled a glass with tap water, Nancy stood. "Is everything in your room okay?"

Elena hugged her arms around her chest. "It's fine."

There was a softness in Nancy Rogers's eyes when she nodded. "It will all be over soon."

Elena tried to take comfort from the officer's words, but found the ominous dread in her would not stop growing. "Yes."

"You're doing the right thing," Nancy said. "Your brother is a monster and he needs to be put away."

Elena had never expected that doing the right thing would be so hard. "It's what must be done."

A sound from the street caught Nancy's attention. "Did you hear something?"

Mendez shut the tap off and set the glass on the counter. He peaked through the kitchen's miniblinds. "Looks like the transfer team arrived early."

Elena's fingers trembled as she pushed back the cuff of her silk blouse and checked the Rolex on her slim wrist. "They're four hours early." She suddenly felt cold, as if Death had brushed past her.

Nancy's hand slid to the holster clipped to her jeans. "I don't like it."

"He's here," Elena whispered as she stepped back. She hated being afraid, being a coward. "He's come to kill me."

Nancy shook her head, puzzled by Elena's words. "Who? Antonio? He's not here."

Elena shook her head, unable to deny the feelings in her. "He's sent people to kill me."

"Don't borrow trouble, Ms. Benito. It could be nothing," Nancy said.

Instinct whispered differently.

Nancy switched off the living-room light and moved past Elena into the dark room. She peeked out of thick curtains covering the picture window. "It makes sense they'd change the schedule. I just wish they'd told us."

There was no tension in Mendez's face when he came into the living room and looked out the same window. A gold signet ring on his pinky caught the moonlight. "Varying the pickup time just means tighter security, Ms. Benito. The car looks like Miami D.A. issue. No need to worry."

Nancy flipped open her cell phone. The light of its screen cast a faint blue light on her angled face. "I'm calling the lieutenant to see if this is legit."

Mendez rubbed the back of his neck. "Man, I hope this gig *is* ending four hours early. I haven't slept in my own bed in two nights and I'm missing my old lady's loving."

Elena stepped back toward her room. She glanced at the side window in her bedroom that led to a back alley.

"Remember the plan," Nancy said to Elena as if reading her thoughts. "If there is any trouble, climb out the window. There is a car parked in the alley. Keys are under the mat and the gas tank is full. Go straight to the central office."

Mendez looked surprised. "Who put the car out back?"

"I did. Just in case," Nancy said.

He cracked his knuckles. "You're so anal, Rogers."

"Better anal than dead, as my brother says," Nancy shot back.

Elena didn't want to be a coward, but raw fear churned in her gut. "Do *you* think it's Antonio?"

Nancy looked calm, too calm, as if she didn't want to spook her witness. She held her phone close to her ear. "Chances are it's like Mendez said. They've changed the pickup time."

Mendez moved toward the door. "You two are worrying over nothing. It's FBI. This time tomorrow Benito will be in—"

Nancy snapped her fingers, signaling Mendez to stop talking as someone came on the line. "Hello, Lt. Grasser, this is Officer Rogers at the Benito safe house. I need a confirmation on an early pickup. We've got men who look like FBI in our driveway now. Right. Okay." She muttered an oath. "The guy put me on hold."

There was a loud knock at the front door. "Mendez and Rogers, open up. FBI."

Mendez looked through the peephole. "He's holding up a FBI badge." He reached for the handle.

"Don't open that door!" Nancy shouted. "Wait until I get a confirmation."

Mendez smiled at his partner.

Elena froze. His was the same oily smile she'd seen on Antonio's face before he'd killed the Churchmen.

Elena felt sick. "He's going to betray us."

Shock registered on Nancy's face but before she could react, Mendez turned the deadbolt.

"Mendez, don't," Nancy shouted.

"I've got to," he said. "There's five million on *her* head and I want it."

The shock on Nancy's face gave way to anger in a split second. Dropping her cell phone, Nancy reached for her gun and shot Mendez in the leg before he could open the door.

"Run!" Nancy shouted to Elena.

Frozen with fear, Elena watched Mendez drop to his knees.

"Bitch." Wincing, Mendez reached for the doorknob.

"Run!" Nancy shouted again to Elena.

Elena did not want to leave the officer behind. She liked the woman and knew if Nancy stayed she'd die.

"Come with me!" Elena begged.

"No," Nancy said. "Now go!"

Elena felt like a coward as she ran into the bedroom. Her high heels caught in the shag carpet and she stumbled to the floor by her bed.

Behind her, she heard the crack of wood splintering as the front door slammed open. Her heart hammering, she kicked off her shoes, rose and ran toward the window. She jerked back the curtains and fumbled with the lock.

Elena glanced back as Nancy swung around, her Beretta raised as three men entered the house. One pulled a sawed-off, double-barreled shotgun from under his black suit jacket. He shot Mendez point-blank in the head. The policeman dropped to the floor, dead.

Nancy fired and hit the shooter in the chest. He fell back into the wall and slid to the floor.

Elena said a silent prayer as she fumbled with the window's lock. She and Nancy had reviewed the escape plan just hours ago, but her thoughts tripped inside her head.

More gunshots exploded in the living room.

The lock gave way and the window opened. Elena hoisted herself up onto the sill and swung her legs over. She jumped the four feet to the soft ground. Bare feet sunk in the moist dirt.

Nancy screamed, firing again. The agonizing sounds tore at Elena. Another shot exploded and then silence.

Elena didn't have to see to know that Officer Nancy Rogers was dead.

Tears clouded her eyes and she ran to the car. Nancy had sacrificed herself for Elena. With trembling hands she opened the car door. The dome light flashed on and she reached under the front mat and got the keys. She immediately closed the door. The vehicle plunged into darkness.

In her rush, she dropped the keys on the floor. Frantically, she ran her hand along the carpeted floor until she felt the cold metal of the keys.

Inside the house, two men entered her room and went to the window out of which she'd just climbed. She shoved the key into the ignition and turned on the engine.

Elena didn't dare look back at the house for fear she'd see them coming. She put the car in Drive and sped down the side street.

Tonight had proven that the five-million-dollar reward on her head was enough to turn anyone against her, including the police. If she showed up at the courthouse later this morning, she would die. Antonio would see to it.

Her heart ached for Nancy. The officer deserved justice. The Churchmen deserved justice.

There was nothing she could do for any of them now but disappear.

Dear Reader,

We hope you enjoyed reading this book. If you did, we'd be so appreciative if you left a review. It really helps us and the author to bring more books like this to you.

Here at HQ Digital we are dedicated to publishing fiction that will keep you turning the pages into the early hours. Don't want to miss a thing? To find out more about our books, promotions, discover exclusive content and enter competitions you can keep in touch in the following ways:

## JOIN OUR COMMUNITY:

Sign up to our new email newsletter: http://smarturl.it/SignUpHQ

Read our new blog www.hqstories.co.uk

https://twitter.com/HQStories

www.facebook.com/HQStories

## BUDDING WRITER?

We're also looking for authors to join the HQ Digital family! Find out more here:

https://www.hqstories.co.uk/want-to-write-for-us/

Thanks for reading, from the HQ Digital team

If you enjoyed *Keep You Close*, then why not try another gripping thriller from HQ Digital?

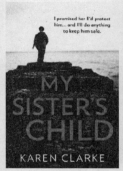

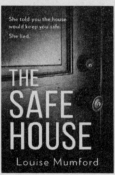